GROWL

STEFAN

NYT AND USA TODAY BESTSELLING AUTHOR

EVE LANGLAIS

Copyright © 2020/2021, Eve Langlais

Cover Art by Yocla Designs © 2020/2021

Title Page by Dreams2Media © 2020/2021

Produced in Canada

Published by Eve Langlais

http://www.EveLanglais.com

Digital ISBN: 978 177384 219 6

Print ISBN: 978 177384 220 2

All Rights Reserved

This book is a work of fiction and the characters, events and dialogue found within the story are of the author's imagination and are not to be construed as real. Any resemblance to actual events or persons, either living or deceased, is completely coincidental.

No part of this book may be reproduced or shared in any form or by any means, electronic or mechanical, including but not limited to digital copying, file sharing, audio recording, email and printing without permission in writing from the author.

PROLOGUE

Smuggling a child from a secret lab in the bright light of day required nerves of steel.

Nanette Hubbard—Nana to her close friends—did her best to fake courage as she drove white knuckled out of Alberta, expecting at any second to see vans with dark-tinted windows come screaming out of nowhere, hemming her in to take back what she'd stolen. A secret they would kill to keep.

The boy she'd rescued spent the first part of that almost twenty-four-hour drive—which she'd driven fueled by caffeine and fear—stretched out on the backseat asleep, his slight frame under the blanket she'd tucked around him. A drug administered by her own brother had put him in a deep slumber, giving her time to get them far away. She stopped only to gas up, and she paid cash while wearing large sunglasses and a wide brimmed hat.

The mud on her license plate changed the look of the letters subtly enough to pass basic scrutiny. As an added precaution, she wouldn't be driving the rental much longer.

When the boy stirred, she knew it was time to finally take a break. She chose the next motel she saw along the highway, the single-story kind with concrete walkways lining the long, skinny building with brightly painted doors. The brackish pool with its chain link fence had caution tape around it. The only other entertainment? A poor excuse for a park.

The motel also included a clerk who really didn't give a hoot who rented a room from him and handed her two almost threadbare towels with a warning she'd be charged for them if they went missing.

Returning to the car, Nana noticed the boy no longer lay on the seat. Panic fluttered at her breast.

Oh no! I've lost him.

As she opened the rear passenger door, she sighed with relief upon seeing him huddled in the footwell.

"Thank goodness you're still here."

He didn't seem as pleased. He eyed her warily.

"Hello, little guy. Remember me?" He might not, given the drugs had already started circulating in his system during their previous brief encounter.

No reply, and that was okay. The world had to be a scary place for the small red-haired boy with an arm in a cast. The breakage was part of the reason he'd been cast aside a little sooner than usual.

They had other excuses, too.

Too puny. Too weak. And his most damning mistake of all? Not being able to shift.

The *huanimorph* project—a stupid play on words that no one could pronounce—was about making humans into something more. And apparently, they had succeeded in some cases.

Those that failed to transform received termination orders.

ST11 was slated for death when her brother, a doctor working under duress, smuggled him out to Nana. She'd loved him the moment she set eyes on him. The feeling wasn't yet mutual.

Nana crouched by the open rear passenger door and held out an apple. Nothing fancy or chock full of preservatives, and yet, his eyes widened. He licked his lips as he stared.

"Would you like to come out of the car?" she asked. She didn't demand. This child had only ever been commanded his scant three years of life.

He didn't reply, and looking into his face, she saw the bruise high on his cheekbone. The wariness in his gaze.

It broke her heart. After living with Dominick—

another rescue and her first smuggled child—she knew better than to cry. Adopting Dominick, and then a year later Pamela, had taught her so much. And broken her, too.

These children had been made to suffer. Knew nothing of love or kindness. Something she could change. Rather than sob and pity them for what they'd endured, she acted and showed these children not everyone was the same. Helped them realize kindness and love existed in the world.

"I've rented us a room," she said, placing the apple on the seat within the boy's reach. She had no intention of using it as blackmail to get him out of the car. He should have the apple because it was the right thing to do.

He eyed the shiny red fruit then her, suspicion causing a crease on his brow.

"I know you won't believe me, but I don't want to hurt you." But she would like to maim the people who'd harmed a child. The first time they met, the boy had been in so much pain, his arm clearly broken and not cared for.

Her brother, Johan, was beside himself. "Mr. X told us to not bother setting the bone." Mr. X being the money and brains behind the secret lab experiments.

"What kind of monster does that?" she'd hissed,

dropping to her knees in front of the child, who flinched from her.

"The kind of asshole who says why bother wasting resources when the subject is only a month away from his third birthday." Johan's voice thickened, upset at the fact this child was supposed to be killed.

In that moment, she wanted to murder her brother. He was a part of this evil, never mind he'd saved Dominick, Pamela, and now this boy. What of all the others kept hidden away? What about the other children?

"I figured that was the case when you called me." She remained eyeing the boy, who stood without crying despite the lines of pain on his face. His solemn gaze met hers. Resignation in their depths. At three years old, did the boy understand what they planned for him?

"Listen to me, ST11." Her brother knelt in front of him. "You have to go with this lady. She's going to take you away to somewhere safe."

"Away?" The word whispered from the child.

"Yes, far away. And you must keep me, this place, your brothers and sisters, a secret."

The boy pressed his lips and nodded. She wanted to scream in frustration. Talk about a heavy secret for one small child to hold.

She stood and glared at Johan. "How can you stay here?"

"They'll kill me if I leave and whoever replaces me might not care." He went to stroke the child's hair but stopped himself.

No affection allowed. It was a rule. One she broke the moment she gained her first two children's trust. Now she had ST11 to convince.

"There must be a way to stop them."

Resignation in his tone, Johan mumbled, "How do you stop something government sanctioned?"

And how to do it in a way that didn't harm the children? They both knew this Mr. X wouldn't hesitate to eliminate them all to cover his tracks.

"I know you're trying." Nana sighed. "It just breaks my heart to know it's happening."

Johan ducked his head. "I'm sorry to drag you into this."

A good thing he had because, otherwise, a different little boy and girl wouldn't be alive today.

"I gave him a sleeping pill," Johan explained. "It won't hurt him but will make it easier for you to travel given his situation."

"You mean his broken arm." Nana trembled, suddenly full of rage. "We have to go."

She didn't hug her brother goodbye.

Despite the pain pulling his features taut, the boy

followed her to the car. Did as told and hid in the back-seat. Nana—a nurse who could have been a doctor—waited until the pill knocked him out and then she set his arm the best she could. Eventually, once he got his identification, she'd have it checked by a real doctor and an x-ray. She couldn't risk it now, not when getting far away and quickly was of paramount importance.

As promised, the boy had slept. She almost dared to believe they'd gotten away safe. Now she just had to convince a small boy to trust her.

She tried a gentle smile. "My name is Nanette Hubbard. But my friends call me Nana. What's your name?"

"ST11."

It was so faint she almost missed it. She smiled. "ST. How mysterious. Is it short for Steven?"

The boy stared at her.

"Hmm. Not Steven. What about Stipplewart? No, too silly. What does ST stand for?" She tapped her chin. "Stew? No, although it is yummy. Wait until you taste mine. Your brother had the initials DK and what do you know, it stood for Dominick, which I would have never guessed."

The boy had reached for the apple as she spoke and took a bite. The way to the heart was always the belly.

She kept talking. "Stewart? Maybe not. Makes me

think of a mouse, and you're not a mouse, are you? More like a lion."

"Tiger."

The word showed he listened to Nana and understood. It also made her realize he must have eavesdropped on his handlers. According to what Johan told her about him, tiger was the strain he'd been crossed with.

She smiled. "I should have known you were a ferocious tiger with that beautiful ginger hair of yours."

Mid chew, he mumbled, "Evil."

"Never!" she exclaimed. Evil would be those who did this to a child.

How could you, Johan? She might kill him yet. But then, who would help her save the children?

The boy ate more apple and, when done, took care of the core.

"I love a good crunchy apple. I've got more in the cooler in the trunk." Packed with a variety of things to feed a growing boy. "I'm going to bring it in the room. Feel free to join me if you'd like."

Rather than crowd him, she gave him the choice. Standing, she headed for the trunk and popped it. She heaved out the cooler, which she carried to the room with its bright yellow door. It matched the ugly flower pattern of the curtains.

The door opened on the expected heavy dark

furniture and patterned carpet. The comforter was more like a quilt with pulled threads all over.

Given the door closed automatically, she used the cooler to prop it open before heading back for the car, only to pause as she saw the boy had crept out of the car, tense and alert. He'd not touched the splint on his arm, and seeing it dangle by his side, she realized she'd need to fabricate a sling.

She knew from her experience with Dominick and then Pamela that it wouldn't take much the first little bit to set him off. They were like wild animals, skittish and ready to run at the first hint of danger. At Dominick's first bolt, she'd cried as she'd searched for him. In the end, he'd returned to her. She'd learned a lot since that time and fallen in love.

The phone calls she'd managed to make to her children on her journey had both her son and daughter exclaiming about missing her tons but the horsies were fun. Nana had both children staying with a friend of hers in Saskatchewan. Just in case things went south with the smuggle, she needed them out of the way. They'd grab Dominick and Pamela on their way back home.

The boy entered the room, and she grabbed the suitcase and bag still in the trunk. She shut all the doors and locked the car. She found ST standing by the jamb, hugging it, eyeing her solemnly. He moved before she could brush past him, tucking between the beds.

"We'll be staying here for a night. I need some sleep." She closed the door gently and then lay a suitcase on the dresser, pulling out items to fit a child his age. She placed them on the bed. "Those are for you. There's a bathroom if you want to bathe or change." She pointed. "Here's some shampoo and soap. Toothbrush, too." She placed the toiletries beside his clothes.

He still hadn't said a word.

She didn't push it. She headed for the television and turned it on, flipping until she found a channel playing children's programming.

Not her preferred method of teaching, however, she needed ST to realize he was in a different world. The quicker he adjusted, the easier he'd fit in. Remaining unnoticed was of paramount importance.

His expression turned comical as he regarded the cartoon antics on the screen of a certain rabbit and a hunter who couldn't seem to bag him.

With the cartoons keeping him riveted, she tackled the cooler, laying out a feast of flavors. Salty cold cuts—ham, chicken, and smoked meat. Cheese —cheddar, Swiss, and mozzarella. Crackers with salted tops. And for the sweet? Grapes, red and green.

The spread brought a shadow, who crept close and watched.

She sat and pointed to the chair across from her. "Care to join me?" She put out a pair of paper plates and began heaping hers.

She held in a smile as she acquired a dinner companion. When they were done, he helped her pack away the cooler, peering curiously inside.

"I have bananas and some instant porridge for breakfast."

"I like bananas." A shy admission.

"Me, too."

She didn't say anything when he followed her to the bathroom. She lay out toiletries, putting a new toothbrush with a superhero on the handle in front of him. Since he was too short to see, she flipped the garbage pail upside down.

"You can stand on that to reach," she indicated. She didn't touch him to help even as she wanted to. He only had one good hand, but as with the other children, he was agile and managed to get on top.

He blinked at his face in the mirror.

She stuck out her tongue, and for a moment, he appeared astonished.

She put toothpaste on their brushes and then proceeded to clean her teeth. He mimicked her. She washed her face with a cloth, and so did he.

When it was time for more private things, she

said, "I have to use the toilet and like to be alone for that if it's okay?"

He nodded and left her presence, even shutting the door all the way. Nana did her business quickly, scared but hopeful as she exited the bathroom.

The boy sat on the floor, watching the television, but turned his head as she appeared. He rose to his feet and said, "Toilet."

"Okay. Be sure to wash your hands when done."

He glanced at his hands. "Okay." He left the door ajar, and so she heard him as he tinkled, flushed, then rinsed his hands at the sink.

When he emerged, she was sitting on the foot of a bed, hands on her lap, trying to look as unthreatening as possible for the talk they had to have.

"How do you feel?" she asked.

He shrugged.

"Are you in pain? I have some medication that might help." Acetaminophen bought for an outrageous price at a gas station. She showed him the bottle.

He bit his lip, the wariness back in his gaze.

"I know things seem kind of strange and scary right now, but I promise I only want to help you. Not hurt. Watch." She poured out the children's medicine into the tiny supplied cup and drank the liquid sweet. "This stuff will help with the pain."

He nodded, and she could have sighed in relief as he took the whole dose.

She kept talking. "Just so you know, we'll only be in this room for the night. Tomorrow, we're back on the road. Two more sleeps and we'll be at the house. I already have a bed for you."

"Me?" He poked himself in the belly.

"Yes, you. And my other son, Dominick, plus my daughter, Pamela. We're all going to live together."

"Doctors?" Just the one word, but it showed what he feared.

"None, unless you need a check-up, but I'll be with you the entire time and if a doctor or anyone tries to hurt you, boom in the kisser." She mimed boxing, and to her delight, the boy laughed.

"Like Bugs." He pointed to the television now turned off.

"Yes, like Bugs. I'm going to take care of you, ST, if you'll let me."

He didn't reply but perked up as she pulled one last surprise for the night. An illustrated book.

"Can I read a story to you?" she asked.

He nodded.

"Let's get you into your pajamas first." She pointed to the clothes. "Would you like me to help?" With his broken arm, his shirt and pants might be tricky.

He nodded and held himself very still as she

worked him out of the travel clothes and into the clean pajamas. The sleeve on the broken side had to be cut open to fit his splinted arm.

He stroked the flannel material covered in dinosaurs. "Soft."

"It is. And so is that bed I'll bet. Can I lift you onto the mattress?" She asked rather than grab him.

He nodded and held out his arms. Carefully, she lifted him onto the bed, tucking him under the sheets.

He uttered a sigh. "Nice."

"It is. Perfect for a bedtime story." She waggled the book to remind him. "But I'll have to sit close if you want to see the pictures."

He scooched away from the edge of the mattress to the middle.

She sat gingerly and put the book in her lap so he could easily see it. She'd stuck to tried and true Dr. Seuss.

By the time she finished reading the silly rhyme, he was cradled against her. When she shut the book, he raised shining eyes to her. "Fun."

"Would you like me to read it again?"

He nodded and halfway through the third repeat, he tilted his head to say, "Stefan."

She immediately knew what he referred to. Didn't know where he heard the name. Didn't ask why he chose it. She simply said, "What a fine name for a strong boy." Her new son.

The following day Stefan met Dominick, a child too wise for his years, who took one look at the broken boy and said, "My brother."

As for Pamela, she hugged him and offered a sloppy kiss that baffled poor Stefan even as he smiled.

Her family had grown. And would continue to grow because of that damned Mr. X.

1

Sometimes having a big family was annoying.

Like now.

"I don't care if Raymond is my brother and some kind of genius, in this he's being an idiot," Stefan grumbled.

"Be nice," Nanette "Nana" Hubbard, aka Mom, admonished.

"I will not be nice. Do you know what that fuckwad asked me to do?" It was a measure of Stefan's agitation that he swore in front of his mom. However, this time, his brother Raymond had gone too far. Before she could reply, he told her. "He wants me to drug myself on catnip and change into my tiger." Because the herb acted as some kind of trigger that turned him from man to beast.

Mom made excuses for Raymond. "He's simply trying to help you and the others figure out what's happening with your bodies."

The reminder pressed Stefan's lips tight. He'd had more than eighteen years to understand he was different. To struggle against the allure of the drug that unleashed his more feral side. "I have no interest in being his guinea pig."

"That's guinea tiger," Raymond drawled, coming out of the basement. More like fucking cave.

"And you must be a vampire cat because you never see daylight." Stefan taunted with the truth. His brother rarely left the house.

"You know my skin is delicate."

"Pussy," Stefan taunted.

"I wouldn't talk Mr. Won't-Give-Any-Blood."

"Keep your needles away from me!" Stefan warned.

"It's just a little prick. You'll barely feel it. I don't need much. And trust me, I wouldn't even be asking if the hair samples gave me what I needed."

That brought a frown to Stefan's face. "What hair samples? I never gave you any."

"Technically, no, and honestly, hair trimmings aren't exactly the greatest."

"You gave him my hair?" He glared at his mother.

"Not exactly," she said with a shrug.

"Don't blame her. If it's on the floor, it's fair game." Raymond's turn to cajole.

"See if I come back," Stefan grumbled.

"You'll be back," his mom predicted. "Because my haircuts are free and come with strawberry rhubarb pie."

He did love Mom's pies. "Fine. But no more letting anyone steal my hair. I'll sweep it up and set it on fire myself if I have to." Anything to annoy his younger brother.

"You can keep your nasty hair. Like I said, it's been useless. I need blood. Preferably from both of your shapes. Speaking of which, when are you going to show it to us?"

"Never." While Stefan had admitted to his secret once he realized Dominick and Tyson had morphed into cats by accident, he'd refused to actually show anyone.

"It would really help with my research."

"If you're so curious, maybe you should be the one chewing down some catnip leaves," Stefan drawled. Because hell yeah, eat enough or smoke enough of the shit, and certain Hubbard family members turned feline. Dominick, Stefan, and Tyson so far. His sister Maeve tried it, but her ursine ass didn't react one bit. Either she remained defective—according to the company who made them—or being a bear, she had a different trigger.

"I can hardly document what's happening if I'm four-legged, you moron."

A good point, but Stefan still didn't agree. "Why aren't you bugging Dominick about this?"

"No need to bug, because he's been cooperating."

Mom jumped in. "My good boy has been doing all kinds of tests for Raymond. Where do you think all those cookies I made went?"

Knowing Dominick, shifting for cookies probably seemed like an easy price. The man would sell his soul for Mom's cooking.

"If you have him helping, then why do you need me?" Stefan knew why, but he felt like whining.

"Because it would be good to know the similarities and differences in the experience. Like, how much does it take before the animal side emerges? How long does it last? Is the dried variety better than liquid, or should you stick to fresh?"

Stefan actually knew the answers to a few. Smoking gave a quicker high. Eating it made it last longer. The liquid stuff gave him the shits.

Rather than tell Raymond, he stuck to, "Find someone else."

"I need a comparison point. Mom won't let me use Tyson. Pammy says she's not in the right place to be fucking with her body right now and, if I asked again, she'd ram my mouse somewhere the sun don't shine." Pammy being one of their sisters. Then there was Maeve, Jessie—who was currently out of town—and Daphne, the youngest. Nine kids in all with the boys, Dominick, Stefan, Raymond, Daeve, and Tyson.

"Tell you what, keep asking and I'll do one better than Pammy and shove your keyboard so far up your ass, you'll burp out the letters," Stefan growled. He knew his brother was purposely trying to agitate him. He actually had a good reason to be asking, Raymond just didn't understand the battle Stefan had waged with the beast. Not the one inside his own body but that of addiction.

"Be nice," Mom admonished. "No fighting amongst each other, not now with the wolves circling." And she meant that quite literally.

"Not with this again." Stefan sighed. Ever since his older brother had a run-in with some local were-wolves—because those fuckers actually existed!—she'd been worried the cats and dogs would erupt into an all-out turf war just like one of her biker shows.

"Wolf packs are territorial," she insisted. "I've been reading up on them."

"They can't be that anal about it, or they'd have known we were here already," he pointed out, despite the fact that in a big city, most people never ran into a fraction of the inhabitants.

"Be that as it may, they know now about us,

which means that invitation we received can't be ignored."

Actually, he'd not just ignored it; he'd set the party invitation on fire a few weeks ago.

"I really don't give a flying rat's ass who they think they are. They keep to themselves. We'll keep to ourselves." To Stefan, it seemed simple. The fewer people that knew about them, the safer they remained.

"I don't think that plan is going to work. This was the reminder I got on my phone today." Mom held up the screen.

Stefan already knew what it would say. *Don't forget the party this Saturday,* with a barbecue emoji. He'd gotten the same message. He imagined they all had.

His advice? "It's an intimidation tactic. Don't reply."

"You want us to ignore the people who had no problem kidnapping Anika?" His mom made it sound like a question and a statement at once.

Anika was his brother's girlfriend, abducted by this so-called wolf pack in order to make Dominick reveal the fact he wasn't human. There'd been much surprise in the family when they realized werewolves existed. Hell, they were still dealing with the after-shocks of their mom's admission all of her kids were actually made in a lab. It explained his intense dislike of needles.

"Would you feel better if I said I'm going to handle it?" Stefan offered.

"How?" she asked.

"Don't worry about it." Try and scare his mom? Two could play that game.

2

Coming out of yoga class, Nimway noticed she was being followed. To give them credit, they were good, and any other girl wouldn't have thought twice about the two seemingly random people shadowing her to her car.

Nimway wasn't just any other girl. As they got near, she whirled. "Can I help you?"

The Girl Scouts looked angelic in their uniforms and perfect smiles, until one saw the evil cookies in their grip. "Would you like to support our troop?" the freckled one lisped. "We have chocolate mint."

"Only the mint?"

"We have more flavors." Out came the catalogue. The girl flipped open to a page where the words coconut and caramel jumped out.

Say no to the cookies. No to doing your civic duty. No to deliciousness.

Nimway bought what they held in their sly arms and put in an order for delivery large enough that her credit card company sent her a text to verify she'd made the purchase.

Yes, goddammit, I bought all the cookies.

Maybe next time she'd be stronger.

Doubtful.

As she headed for her car, she noticed a motorcycle parked alongside it, its driver perched on the metal bumper separating the vehicles from the attempt at greenery in the asphalt parking lot. The visor hid their features, but the leather jacket molded broad shoulders. This close, he smelled faintly of exhaust, a crisp cologne that didn't annoy, and something else.

Yummy.

It perked her interest, which meant she kept a cautious ear on him, listening for movement as she reached for the handle on her car. The fob in her purse unlocked it automatically.

Not that she worried about handling one guy.

As she pulled the door open, he stood and pulled off his helmet. "Hello, Nimway Pendraggun of the Valley Pack."

She really needed to do something about the

name. Her parents had a fetish for all things Arthurian. It didn't extend to research or spelling.

She turned to face the tall fellow with the red hair pulled back from his face and a rather splendid beard. "Do you really want to do this here and now, Stefan Hubbard?" She'd seen his file and his picture. She knew all about him and his odd family. Nine plus mom. At least two of them confirmed shifters. Hmmm, make that three.

This close, the scent was distinctive. Not human. Not wolf either. His brother was a cat. She'd wager Stefan Hubbard was as well. Never mind the fact only werewolves were supposed to exist. It had recently been brought to her attention that some people had been dabbling in human experiments. Was it any wonder the pack was in an up-growl, demanding their alpha do something about it?

His brow arched. "Should I be flattered you know who I am?"

"Actually, you should be concerned. It's not every day we discover a family of potential rivals under our very noses." In her mind, the Hubbards posed a threat. First and foremost because one sloppy move on their part could expose everyone. And second, they were cats in wolf territory.

The only good news? Even if the entire family could shift, they lacked the numbers to rival the pack. Despite that, their existence in the valley proved problematic.

The packs scattered around the world had rules about borders and who could live within them. To keep authority, and power, one had to enforce the rules, which meant a pretty final destination. Which was why the pack had been debating what to do with the Hubbard family. Most wanted to run them out of town.

She didn't get the feeling Stefan would like that option.

He held his helmet in one hand, dangling down by his leg. His jeans molded his slim physique. His height came from his long legs. His expression held a firmness to it as he snapped, "What the fuck are you yapping about? Despite my ride, we're not some kind of gang looking to move into your territory."

She stepped closer to him and looked up, way up, and took in his scent before whispering, "Are you really going to try and lie to me? We both know you're more than human." Not a conversation they should be having in a parking lot, and yet, where else could they go? At least they were alone, and in a neutral spot.

"You're mistaken."

"What did I say about lying?" she chided, tapping his cheek. "Your scent doesn't lie. It's definitely feline."

"Maybe I just own a cat."

"It's not the same, and you know it." She clucked her tongue. "Stop pretending. I know you can shift. I just don't know into what kind of kitty. Maybe if we went to a zoo, I could sniff around and figure it out." The closest one she knew with big cats was in Toronto.

"I'm afraid you're mistaken."

Another lie, but having read his file with his history of addiction, it hit her. "Do you have to get high to shift?"

"I got high because I liked it."

"Not according to your records. You were prescribed medication for depression on numerous occasions. Did you have a hard time accepting your other side?"

For a moment, he appeared to struggle before harshly exclaiming, "What do you think? Most teenagers only have to deal with hair on their balls. Try hair all over your body and blackouts."

So much now made sense. "The discovery you could shift is why you were in and out of rehab for addiction so much in your teens and early twenties. You couldn't handle discovering you weren't like other boys. And I'll bet when you told the truth, people called you crazy."

"I never told anyone," he mumbled. "I knew they'd never believe me."

"Not even your family?"

That had him scuffing the ground in discomfort, and she really expected him to not reply, but to her surprise, he had a soft admission. "Tell my family I was a freak? Nope. Instead I let them think I was a crackhead." He lifted his head and offered a wry, "Because that was so much better."

"It must have been fucked up to realize your family shared that trait." She coaxed him, knowing at one point he'd realize he'd said too much and shut down. He didn't seem the type to spill his guts.

"I see what you're doing. Trying to get me to admit shit." He scowled. "I did not come here for you to try and head-shrink me."

"Don't act pissy because I'm easy to talk to," she hotly retorted. And probably one of the weirdest things she'd ever said. Most people usually avoided conversations with her. Something about her being intimidating.

"Who said it was easy? You're just tricking me into saying stuff."

"Then don't reply. It's not like I'm twisting your arm, baby."

"Don't fucking call me baby. I didn't come here to give you my life story but to tell you to back off."

"No can do. It's my job to scout out potential rivals."

His brows rose. "How are we rivals? For Christ's

sake, we're not interested in taking anything from you."

"Yet. What about once your numbers grow?"

Stefan snorted. "I can assure you my family has no plans to conquer Ottawa if that's what you're asking."

According to the file, none of them had interesting jobs with the government or in other influential areas. Which was just plain shortsighted. The pack always had people in a few key spots, like law enforcement, the judicial system, and even on city council. They'd been strong advocates for more off-leash parks. A young wolf could pass for a dog easily enough and needed a place to expend their energy.

"That's not the only concern. Your presence could expose us."

"How?"

"For one, your brother was sloppy when he shifted and seen by a human. His story made the news."

Stefan grimaced. "A mistake that won't happen again."

And yet it had, leading them to hunt Dominick down. Which was when the pack made an error. "You know what we are."

"Because *your* people showed us. Otherwise, we'd have gone on thinking we were freaks that shouldn't exist."

"Oh, you shouldn't exist," she said flatly. The experiment that twisted him into a feline was a human-made genetic change based off the lycanthrope ability. Or so they'd learned. The details remained murky, as did the people behind the project.

"Harsh, but true," he admitted. "Which is why we just want to stay out of sight."

She waved a hand. "Go right ahead. Just don't do it in our territory. Your family will have to relocate." She poked him to see if he'd capitulate. As expected, he didn't.

"I don't give a shit what you or your pack wants. We are not moving." He sounded firm on that point.

"Is that a threat?"

He cocked his head. "We're not looking for a fight. But I get the impression you are."

"It's called looking after the pack. Its survival is my number one priority. And if you pose a threat to it, then what you want doesn't matter." Cold, but true. Everyone remembered the story that came out of Russia in the eighties. A wolf clan, thirty strong, wiped out but for one teenage boy. Humans weren't kind to those they considered monsters. It only made sense to strike first.

The low whistle went with his headshake. "Fuck me, but that's aggressive. So should I expect my family to get picked off one by one since we're enemy number one?"

"Not yet. We're still coming to a decision, which is why your family received an invitation to present themselves." Her brother's idea. As pack alpha, Gwayne had decided the Hubbard family should have a chance to make an impression at the Fall Family Barbecue. A yearly tradition that put the cooks of the families in competition against each other with delicious results. She couldn't wait for Aunt Jenny's ribs and Uncle Pete's caramel-drizzled apple pie.

"You can't seriously expect us to show up." Apparently, Stefan didn't understand what a grand gesture the invitation was. Outsiders never got invited.

"Did I mention you don't have a choice?"

"Hell yeah we do. No way is my family going anywhere near you psychos, not after what you did."

"Don't tell me you're going to whine about what happened?" She rolled her eyes.

"You kidnapped my brother's girlfriend."

"And gave her back unharmed." Mostly because they'd proved a point and satisfied a curiosity. There were shifters on their land, and they needed to be reined in. But carefully, so as to not draw notice. Already the Hubbard clan had been careless, and the Valley Pack had their best scrubbing the internet of every unfortunate mention of the animal attack.

He snorted. "Unharmed? I heard what happened that night. You were going to hurt Anika if Dominick didn't confess to being a panther."

"We just wanted him to tell the truth. And luckily, he did, with a plausible enough excuse for his ignorance. Had he lied, we wouldn't have spared his life."

Stefan's eyes widened. "You would have killed my brother?" Finally, she'd managed to startle him.

"This isn't a game, baby. The pack's survival is the only thing of importance, and anyone who gets in the way of it..." She canted her head and smiled.

"You're admitting to murder."

"Who are you going to tell?" she taunted. "No one because you have too much to hide."

"Don't get too cocky there, *darling*."

Was that retaliation for baby? How delicious.

"Tell me about your family. Nine kids. All adopted. From where?" Because the adoption papers led to a dead end. The only reason they even knew about the lab thing was because Gwayne had been in contact with one of the Hubbards.

"How about you answer a few questions instead? Dominick says your pack can change into wolves."

For a second, she almost didn't answer. He wasn't pack. How dare he question?

And yet, he intrigued her, mostly because it

seemed impossible he knew nothing. "All lycans can shift."

"You too?" he specified.

"I am a wolf shifter, and I would advise you right now to never say bitch."

"Duly noted. How did you become a wolf?"

Her brow arched. "Baby, I was born this way."

"So was I but not without some scientific help. Were you also created in a lab?"

She saw the moment he realized he'd spilled too much, and he tried to fix his error. "Test tube pregnancy." He tried to make light of it, but she became a wolf with a bone and held on.

"I already know your origin story. See, we had some questions when we realized you were never legally adopted. Being created in a secret lab explains why we couldn't find anything about you or the rest of your family. The question being, have those you were stolen from given up looking?" she mused aloud. "I wonder if there's a reward for your return."

Panic flitted across his face. "You can't expose us."

She'd never do it, but she wasn't about to admit it. "It would solve the pack's problem." A cruel barb that took the panic and turned it into anger.

"I'd be careful tossing that kind of threat around, because I'll bet they'd be interested in natural-born huanimorphs."

"Say what?"

He waved a hand. "It's a stupid word for what they were trying to create. Human-animal hybrids."

"I'd say they succeeded. Who's doing the creating?" Because their Hubbard source didn't have the slightest clue.

"How the fuck would I know? I escaped there when I was a kid. And I won't go back." He looked agitated as he slapped his helmet off his leg. He glanced at her. "They're the reason you don't have to worry about us doing anything to draw attention."

"Except you already have. Or have you forgotten about the man your brother put in hospital?"

Dominick had clawed a human instead of killing him outright. The man told everyone what he saw, which led to complications.

"He didn't mean to do it. The animal thing, it's hard to control."

"No, it's not," she said with a frown.

"You trying to say your pack wolves don't ever run off and attack people?"

"We hunt game in the woods, not people."

"How can you be sure you haven't? Haven't you ever woken up from a morph and wondered where the blood came from?"

She stared at him, and understanding clicked into place. "Are you saying when you shift, you don't control the body?"

His lips pressed into a line.

"And let me guess, like your brother, you require catnip to change." She'd not believed it at first; however, their source insisted that the shift didn't work without a catalyst.

"So what? You must use something, too. What is it, wolfsbane?"

She didn't react to the word. "We use nothing to shift."

"Then how do you do it?"

"We just do. Some of us are better at it than others. The weak require moonlight to help. The strong can do it at will and sometimes more than once in a short period of time."

"At will." He said it musingly.

"Yes, at will. And you should be able to as well. Shifting is a part of you. You shouldn't need an herb at all."

"Guess again, darling. Without it, nothing happens."

The news had her muttering, "Interesting. Is your entire family the same way?"

He frowned and sidestepped the question. "Is that really what it's called, shifting?"

She patted his cheek. "You have so much to learn."

"Then teach me."

She paused as she was getting into her car to

shoot him a glance. "Now there's something I bet you don't say often."

"I mean it. You obviously know more about this shifting thing than me. I need a teacher." Gone was the arrogance.

She chuckled. "You definitely don't want me." She lacked patience, which was why Gwayne led the pack and not her.

"How else am I supposed to figure out what's happening?"

"You want answers? Then I'll see you at the barbecue."

Where the fate of Stefan and his family would be decided.

3

Stefan had admitted too much, and he wasn't even sure why. It certainly wasn't because Nimway had a warm and inviting personality.

Abrupt. Confidant. Sexy. With a way of making him spill his darkest secrets.

Ugh.

Meeting Nimway hadn't solved shit. Nope. Now Stefan had more questions than ever, such as, would her lips taste as good as they looked?

She'd probably gut him if he tried to find out. They'd not gotten off on the best foot. He'd tracked her down since she seemed to be easier to approach than her brother. Gwayne lived in Barrhaven, of all places, in a neighborhood with good schools and parks.

A werewolf in suburbia? It seemed farfetched,

but then again, what did he know? Until recently, he'd thought himself the only transforming freak in the family until the incidents with Dominick and Tyson. Odd that he'd talked more about his condition with Nimway than his own brothers. Why had he spilled his guts to her?

Just call him Captain Caveman. Why, he'd even divulged the shameful fact that he didn't know how to control the beast. For a while, he'd been convinced he must be a serial murderer given how many times he'd woken in the woods with animal parts strewn around. Only once had he been dumb enough to puke. After that exorcist-style projectile vomiting of chunks best left hidden, he learned to swallow back the nausea. Eventually, he got to the point he was licking his lips.

Enjoying the carnage? Not the last straw before he got help. But close. It took something worse to send him to a clinic to dry out.

Not once in more than a decade had he been tempted to let that other side of him out. He had the tiger locked away. Safe.

But then Nimway claimed he should still be in control, that it was possible to drive the beast. Could that ability be taught? Problem being she had no interest in helping him. Rather, she'd prefer to run him and his family out of town.

Not happening, but at the same time, he didn't want to bend a knee. Leaving what choice?

She'd told him to meet her at the party. If he went, would she give him answers? Could he afford to stubbornly stay away and not find out more?

Only one thing to do when faced with a tough decision. Talk it out with the one person he trusted —the person he should have told his secret sooner.

Stefan ended up on a stool at his mom's kitchen island, hugging a mug of her special tea, creamy and thick with a hint of sugary spice. Add in the salted and candied walnuts, plus the freshly sliced cured meat, and he slowly calmed. Chewing could do that for a person.

At this point in the snack, he'd already told his mom about the meeting with Nimway. But that wasn't the thing she really wanted to know about.

"When are you going to talk to me about your tiger?"

He choked on his mouthful of tea. He grabbed a napkin and managed a husky, "How's never?"

"Why?"

"Because it's the reason I struggled and hit the drugs hard." He offered her a wan smile. "Pretty sure neither of us wants to relive those years."

"Even during that rough patch, you were still a good boy." She reached out and grabbed his hand.

"I was an addict with attitude." He'd lashed out

40

at his family, thinking himself too different to be worthy of their love. Afraid at the same time he might inadvertently hurt them.

"You were a huge ass, but you seem to forget that the only person you ever hurt was yourself."

The ancient monks flagellated with reeds and leather strips, whatever they could find. Stefan emotionally shredded himself with brutal fierceness. "I was out of control."

"But it wasn't just the drugs," she surmised. "It was also because you found out about your other side."

He fidgeted. "Not exactly. I didn't know at first what was happening to me. The blackouts made sure of that."

"When did it start?"

"I was sixteen and sleeping over at Billy's. He had a cat." Who'd dropped a catnip toy by his head.

The next morning, his friends mocked him when they discovered him sprawled naked with it in his mouth. Even as he fled their mockery, he craved the catnip. That same day, he ended up in the pet store for more of the green powdery stuff. And the snowball down the hill began.

"Did you morph in front of Billy?" Mom exclaimed.

"Not exactly. There wasn't enough for a full shift. Just enough to get a high and be stupid."

A cheap high, which meant when he went from just sniffing to smoking it, he could do a shit-ton at once. It led to blackouts and waking up naked. Sometimes with blood and hair in his mouth, the remains of whatever animal he'd killed sometimes tucked close by.

For a while, he assumed he must be a psychopath. Back then, cell phone videos were a new thing, so he had to borrow a camera to record what happened. He set it to go off at motion then got high in the woods. He smoked it and even chewed down some of it. Crunchy. Tasty.

He actually woke up in the same place he'd gotten wasted, not wearing any clothes, the remains of a fish stinking up his bed of moss. And when he later replayed the camera video, he'd almost keeled over.

A tiger. He turned into a fucking tiger!

Stefan didn't even realize he'd told his story until Mom said, "You idiot. Why didn't you talk to me?"

He glanced at her. "Because I thought there was something wrong with me. Worried I was dangerous. I was. *Am*," he corrected himself.

"Have you killed anyone?"

"Not that I know of." He'd watched the news for reports of wild animal attacks.

"Then not sure what the problem is."

He blinked at his mom. "The problem is I turn

into a striped menace with no thought other than hunting."

"Hunting animals. It's not like you're a vegan."

"Not the same, Mom."

"Bow and arrow, gun, or teeth. All weapons. Yours are just more portable now."

He just about choked as she justified him being a furry killing machine. "I hope you haven't said that to Tyson."

She snorted. "And encourage him? No. But, he does need someone who's dealt with this particular problem to guide him. I'll bet Dominick wouldn't mind a word either."

His brothers had both come to him for advice. He'd told them to stay away from catnip. "I'm not sure my failures can be of any help."

"Says the man who kicked the habit. How many years now?"

"Coming up on a decade." But it came with a price. He was always tense, snarly if people got in his way. Exercise and fucking were the only things that gave him relief. And the latter had been losing its appeal. He could hardly sleep for more than an hour or two anymore, and women didn't like it when you left them in the middle of the night.

A tray of cookies slid out of the oven. Coconut macaroon and almond chunk. Mom would now drizzle chocolate on top, which would harden, making it the perfect treat.

He waited patiently for it. Always had, even as a little boy. Dominick, his older brother, had tried to teach him to steal one when Mom turned her back, but Stefan relied on patience. It always earned him a treat, although Mom claimed it was his eyes that made her weak.

Mom no sooner finished pouring chocolate than his sister Maeve walked into the kitchen and grabbed one. Didn't even ask. Her short pixie cut was a vivid pink with streaks of pure white. She wore it well, along with some silver studs in her ears, nose, and eyebrow.

"Aren't you brave?" Stefan taunted. Dominick got his hand smacked every time he tried the same.

"Don't need bravery because I'm Mom's favorite," Maeve crooned. His younger sister still lived at home.

"You wish," he huffed.

"I have no favorites, and Maeve gets a cookie because she's too skinny. She needs to eat more," Nana declared.

Maeve snorted. "For the last time, I am not underweight. Stefan, on the other hand, looks like he's been hitting the lasagna hard."

"I am not fat!"

"If you say so. Shirt must have shrunk in the wash."

He might have gained a few pounds, but an extra hour in the gym would fix that. "And to think I once beat up that nice ice cream man because he called you a name." Stefan might have been more patient than Dominick when it came to certain things, but he didn't tolerate any bullying of his siblings.

"Ha, you didn't do that for me. As I recall, after you had that *talk* with him"—she flipped some fingers to air quote—"you got free Dilly Bars until he changed jobs."

He smiled. "I do love Dilly Bars."

"And my cooking." His mom beamed, handing him a plate with four cookies, making him wonder, how much was a normal serving?

He glanced down. "Maybe I should cut down on my carbs."

"Nonsense," scoffed his mother.

Maeve had different advice. "When you get changed into your nice clothes, don't tuck your shirt in; it will be less noticeable."

"Why am I getting changed?" He played dumb.

"You know the barbecue is tomorrow night."

"And? I don't recall it saying I had to dress up."

"We are not going there looking like bums," his mom declared.

"There is no we and no party. I won't have this family going anywhere near that group."

Maeve clapped. "Bravo, oh mighty savior who thinks he talks for all of us."

"Don't start with me," he growled. "I don't want you involved in this."

"Already am, or have you forgotten I was born in the same lab?" Maeve said with a lilt in the reply.

He closed his eyes. He didn't need the reminder. "But you haven't been able to change."

"Not for lack of trying. Catnip doesn't work on bears."

"I don't know why you'd even want to. Doesn't it freak you out?" Stefan exclaimed.

"While I am not crazy about the idea of wearing a flea collar, I actually think it's kind of cool. If I can ever figure out my trigger."

"You might be lucky and not have the gene that makes you into an animal," he suggested.

"Oh, I am pretty sure I do because it would explain the time I had a blackout after a one-night stand. I thought he roofied me when I woke naked in the park the next day. In retaliation I keyed the shit out of his car."

He winced. "Ouch."

She shrugged. "Honest mistake."

"Do you know what triggered it?"

She shook her head. "Nope, but Raymond's got

some ideas we can try to figure out."

"I really wish you'd slow down on the testing," Mom grumbled. "It's dangerous."

"Mom's right. You shouldn't treat this lightly," Stefan declared.

"Exactly, which is why we need to know more. Mom thinks there will be people at this party that might be able to give us some answers."

"I don't trust them."

"I should hope not," Maeve replied. "We barely know them. But the only way to find out what kind of people they are is to get close to them."

He had gotten close to one. She reminded him of catnip in that he didn't feel himself around her.

"We are going tomorrow night," his mom stated. "All except for the youngest."

"Meaning Maeve, too?" he taunted.

"Ha. Ha. Funny. Not." His sister grimaced. "Actually, I'm going to talk to Pammy and see if I can convince her to come."

"Is she talking to us yet?" Pamela had a minor meltdown after the revelation they'd been created in a lab and spliced with animals. She claimed she needed time to think about it and distanced herself. He had a feeling he knew what that meant.

"She's just sorting through some stuff right now. With work. And her love life." Mom looked concerned.

He made a mental note to check in on Pamela. "I don't think she should go. And neither should you or anyone else in this family."

Mom shook her head. "I'm going."

"Me too!" Maeve chimed in.

"This is a bad idea."

"It might be, so the question is, will you be by my side keeping me safe? Or let me enter the den of wolves alone?" Mom laid it on thick.

He groaned. "For fuck's sake, fine, I'll go. But I'm not staying long."

Maeve exploded her fingers as she exclaimed, "Kaboom, taken out by the guilt monster."

"Not funny," he grumbled. "Let it be known I am against this dumbass idea."

"Don't be so negative. Maybe you'll find someone at this party."

Stefan couldn't believe she said it. "Mom, I am not looking for a girlfriend."

"You should. You are getting up in years."

He tugged on his beard. "Mom!"

Maeve cackled. "Old and fat. Better hurry up and get married."

He glared at his sister. "Still not amusing."

Mom agreed. "Finding the perfect partner is serious work, which is why you'll be on your best behavior, Maeve Hubbard."

"Hold on a second. Why are you talking to me?" Maeve squawked.

"You could use someone in your life."

"I'm not even thirty."

"And? Love can hit at any time. There will be boys at this party," Mom sang.

"Mom, we're talking about werewolves at this party. I'm a bear. Definitely not compatible."

"You don't know that for sure," Mom interjected.

"Take one for the team, Maeve," he teased his sister.

"Shut up," Maeve hissed.

"Ah, now, don't be shy. You have permission from Mom to get knocked up."

"Speaking of knocking up, Henny at the beauty shop has a niece only a year younger than you. Single. Attractive. Works full time at Home Depot as a manager."

He blinked at his mom. "No."

"Don't answer yet. You haven't even seen her."

He shook his head. "I am not getting hooked up with anyone." He almost added ever. With the bomb he carried around inside, he didn't dare take the chance.

His brother Dominick had, though. He was engaged to the very human Anika. Didn't he worry about what he might pass on?

"You say that now. But wait until you meet the

right lady." His mom clasped her hands. "You never know when true love will hit." Mom had only loved one man in her life, and he died a year before she adopted her first orphan.

"On second thought, maybe I'll stay home."

"Do it, you pussy," Maeve dared, popping a cookie into her mouth. "Stay home and pretend none of this is happening. The rest of us are going to meet the neighbors. Fingers crossed I don't insult them."

"Or else what? The wolves won't invite us back?" was his sarcastic reply.

"They might choose to rid their territory of those they see as rivals."

He would have called it an exaggeration except for his conversation with Nimway. "They better not harm my family."

Maeve shrugged. "You won't be there to stop it from happening, so here's to hoping none of us do something stupid while you're pouting at home."

Before he could reply, his mom jumped in. "It's fine, Stefan. If you are that opposed, you should stay away. Don't worry. We'll have Dominick with us."

That hotheaded Neanderthal? He groaned, succumbing to the reverse psychology. "I'm going, but I'm not dressing up."

But he did wear a special T-shirt.

4

Mom stared at Stefan's shirt, while Tyson outright laughed. Dominick shook his head and said, "You trying to get us killed?"

"What's wrong with it?" Stefan glanced down at the image of sexy Red Riding Hood, cloak and skirt hiked high to reveal a leg, wagging a finger at a wolf. The text beside her read: *Eat me.*

"The purpose of this endeavor is to force a peaceful alliance, not piss them off. And you know that means you're just being a dick." Dominick, as usual, provided a blunt opinion.

A correct one as it turned out. Stefan was being unusually contrary. He couldn't help himself. He'd been feeling more antsy than usual since meeting Nimway. Still, his family had a point. He shouldn't purposefully antagonize their hosts. "Anyone got a shirt handy?" He'd moved out years ago and didn't keep any spare clothes on hand.

With Raymond having only two-collar shirts, and the other one red—something his ginger ass wouldn't tolerate—he got stuck with something from Dominick's closet, an oversized, button-up plaid. His brother grinned as he slung an arm around him.

"Twins."

"Fuck off."

"Chin up, little brother," Dominick teased. "Now that I'm a taken man, maybe you'll have a chance with the ladies."

"Not interested in catching fleas."

"Don't my boys look handsome. Smile." Mom had her damned phone up and was clicking away. He didn't know what for since she didn't use social media. Perhaps she had massive cloud storage where she kept all their pictures in anticipation of a future wedding slideshow to torture guests. "Let's get going." She swept out the door.

"In a second," Dominick said. "I wanna tell Pammy we're going."

"Pretty sure she already knows," tittered Maeve, bouncing down the stairs and outside.

While Pammy hadn't answered any calls or texts to say whether she was going to the barbecue, she did reply when Stefan fired her a message that said simply, *Someone should watch the kids while we're out.* Sixteen-year-old Tyson and nine-year-old Daphne were too young for the visit.

Tyson wasn't happy about it, and he glowered at them from a spot halfway up the stairs. "It's not fair. I should be allowed to go. You're treating me like a baby."

"You want me to treat you like a man?" Dominick grabbed the kid by the back of the neck and reeled him close. "You are the man of the house the moment we leave. Something happens to your sisters while we're gone, and we will blame you."

Big eyes blinked.

Dominick smiled with too many teeth to be friendly. "We clear?"

Tyson nodded and swallowed hard.

"Bravo," Stefan muttered, clapping. "And in case it wasn't clear, ditto to what he said."

They then yelled good-bye to Daphne, who was already scanning the horror movie channel, which had Tyson gulping. "She's too young for that, right?"

"I'm sure you'll reassure her if she gets scared." Stefan clapped his brother on the back before he left.

While Stefan had ridden his bike to the farm-house, Mom had already told him he'd be riding with the family in one of two vehicles. His luck, he ended up in the passenger seat of the minivan, a baby blue vehicle with a stick family running from a dinosaur in the rear window. Raymond, Anika, and Dominick sat in the back two rows. Maeve, having plans for later, insisted on driving her Jeep and took off like a purple bat out of Hell.

Not so the minivan. Mom drove and stuck to the speed limit. It gave them too much time to talk.

"Any idea how many people will be at this party?" Dominick asked.

"Enough that we'll be in trouble if someone steps out of line." Mom's warning came with a flash of her eyes in the rearview mirror, ensuring everyone felt the glare.

"I'd listen to Mom and think twice about causing trouble." Raymond had taken the third row of seating and had a laptop balanced on his knees—not the kind bought in a store. He'd modified it to his use.

"Mama's boy," Stefan coughed.

"More like smart one. I've been searching this Valley Pack group."

"Searching what? I highly doubt the local were-wolves are advertising their presence," Stefan drawled with a hint of sarcasm.

"No, but digging into the address we're visiting brought up some interesting items. Such as the fact a company labeled The LVP owns Gwayne Pendraggun's house. As a matter of fact, LVP has bought many houses in this neighborhood via many shell companies in the past few years, which I'll admit took some serious digging to discover."

"Meaning they're coordinated, with money," Anika pointed out.

"How many houses we talking about?" Dominick asked.

Raymond had a ready answer. "Try more than fifty."

Dominick whistled. "That's a lot of wolves."

"If they're all able to morph," Stefan retorted. Nimway had acted as if it were a given. He still had his doubts.

"Even if they can't, they might possibly pass on that gene to their children." Mom's contribution as she stopped well before the light turned yellow to the annoyance of the car following.

"What makes you think that?" Stefan didn't follow the logic.

It was Raymond who said, "Because the houses they bought are single-family homes. We're talking three and four bedrooms with yards and double driveways with garages."

"Good for them. They want to have puppies in suburbia." He couldn't have said why he remained acerbic. "It still doesn't mean shit to us, given they're in Barrhaven with plenty of room to expand." Mom's house was in Richmond, southwest of where the wolves had taken up residence.

"I don't think it's about expansion, but protection," Mom interjected. "In the wild, predators tend to stake out territory and then maintain its boundaries. It's to create a safe haven for the breeding females and young."

"We're not animals," Stefan barked.

"No, but you're also not just human either, my dear son. Some of your motives might be driven by that specialness inside you."

"Maybe that explains my urge to mark my condo with piss." Sarcasm was his method of coping, but his family didn't always appreciate it.

"If you can't say anything constructive, shut the fuck up," Dominick snapped.

"Yes, Daddy." Stefan couldn't stop himself.

"I know you're picking a fight in the hopes I'll dump you on the side of the road and spare you this party. I will stop if you want me to. Just ask," Mom said.

"You know I don't want to go." Even though he couldn't explain why. "But I have to. I can't let you face this by yourself." He'd never get answers, such as the one that burned the most. How to make the hidden tiger within go away forever?

"Just try not to be an asshole," Dominick grumbled. "Which reminds me, no seducing any wives at the party, Stefan."

"Why are you singling me out? What about Ray?

Or Mom? Have you seen what she's wearing?" He'd noticed the rarely seen eyeshadow and jewelry.

"Don't deflect. We both know they're not the ones with a history of doing it," Dominick reminded.

"It was only the one time." And it got ugly, as the married woman left her husband, expecting them to get together.

She thought wrong.

Before Stefan could reply, Mom glared at him. "You cuckolded someone?"

"She seduced me," Stefan exclaimed.

"You could have said no," Mom hissed. "I didn't raise you to be a home-wrecker. How would you feel if it happened to you?"

"Never going to happen because I am never getting married. Ever." Stefan remained adamant on that point.

Dominick chuckled. "Never say never. Look at what happened to me."

"Your stalking paid off," muttered Anika, which drew even more laughter.

"I don't know why you're both so against the idea. I'd get married." Raymond kept typing as he joined the conversation.

"You'd have to leave the basement for that to happen," Stefan teased.

"Leave him alone. Raymond will meet the right girl when the time is right," Mom declared.

"Why does he get to wait and I don't?" Stefan growled.

"Because you're closer to forty. Everyone knows a man who doesn't marry before forty is doomed to be single and die younger than his married friends." Mom and her damned proclamations.

"Bullshit." Yet he wondered, was it true? Dammit. He'd have to ask Raymond to research it later when Mom couldn't hear him asking. "Nothing wrong with being single. I'd hate to share my closet."

"I've seen your closet. It has no room for anyone else. Tiger my ass. I think you might be a peacock." Dominick flapped his arms like wings and made a screech that almost sent Stefan diving between the seats.

"You're just jealous because I have style."

"A man doesn't need more than two pairs of shoes. His everyday pair and his good pair." Dominick snorted.

"Slippers are the most important footwear," was Raymond's contribution from the back. His brother had a thing for moccasins, which drove Stefan nuts.

"You don't get to speak about style. I've seen the state of your T-shirts." Stefan shuddered

"It's known as vintage," Raymond intoned.

"He's got a point. Old is in," Dominick agreed.

Mom chose Stefan's side. "A rag is a rag."

"Thank you!" Stefan exclaimed.

All the bantering meant they had almost arrived. At a traffic light, Mom leaned over and patted his cheek. "Remember to smile pretty at the ladies."

"Yeah, Stef, smile. And bat those lashes," Dominick teased.

Stefan bared his teeth. "How's this?"

"Stop bugging your brother. It wasn't too long ago you were being an idiot. It's a wonder Anika puts up with you."

"It's not easy." Anika's dry reply.

"Are you sure you're healthy? Sane? Or is he paying you to pretend to like him? Because I don't get it." Stefan lived to bug Dominick.

"You leave those two alone. At least he managed to get a girlfriend, while you continue to waste your life and seed away."

Stefan choked. "Mom!"

"Don't think I haven't heard about your antics," his mom chided.

"All consensual."

"How about trying to make one of your conquests full time so you don't need testing every other week?"

It was monthly, actually, and he used protection. "Why are you harassing me? I don't hear you saying shit to Raymond, even though this is only the second time he's left the house in the last two weeks.""

"Raymond is shy."

"Raymond is a pussy who hides behind a computer screen all day."

"Making big bucks at it, too!" Raymond retorted, barely lifting his head. The man was always fiddling with something electronic. Had been since they were kids and Mom got him his first computer. He'd been bullied in school, and Mom opted to have him learn from home.

"I'm working on some ideas for Raymond. But you…" She huffed. "You need a firm hand."

Odd how he suddenly pictured Nimway, a woman not easily cowed. He'd not stopped thinking of her since their meeting. Thought of what he'd say when he ran into her again. Because he had no doubt he would. Looked forward to it even. Craved it with an excitement once reserved for Christmas morning.

What the fuck was wrong with him?

5

THE SUDDEN PANIC WAS VERY REAL. STEFAN opened his mouth to tell Mom to let him out.

Too late.

"We're almost there." Mom turned off Eagleson into a neighborhood with houses crowded too close together. It made him claustrophobic. He blamed sharing a room with two brothers growing up.

As they prowled the residential road with its *Watch the Children* signs, he noticed nothing odd until they turned onto the street they were looking for. For one, it had more than a few couples pushing strollers or walking hand in hand, seemingly perfect, until they turned their heads as if on a possessed pivot to stare at them as they drove by.

"What's up with the people?" Dominick asked, letting Stefan know it wasn't his imagination.

"How many members did you say this pack had?" Because Stefan had already counted eighteen that he would wager were part of the group.

"Well, do the math. Fifty houses, probably one to two adults per household... At least a hundred, maybe more?" Raymond said.

"All werewolves?" Anika asked, frowning out the window.

"Unless they're inbreeding, you gotta figure some are married to humans. I'll have to run backgrounds on the names to see." Raymond kept tapping away at his laptop.

Stefan couldn't hold his tongue. "How do you not already have this information? You've had since Thanksgiving." Just under a week ago, which was usually long enough for Raymond to dig up the dirt.

"I've been busy."

"With what? What could be more important than a threat to this family?" Stefan demanded.

"Maybe you're not curious, but I want to know who was behind the lab. Who made us? Why?" It stunned Stefan to realize what his brother had been seeking. Information about their pasts. Their origin. Because it turned out they were not simple orphans. They'd been created in a lab. Experiments. Failures. Defective versions slated for death.

Dealing with it might take time and some AA

meetings because he could feel himself craving something to quell his sudden anxiety.

It was Dominick who dared to ask, "Did you find anything?"

"Nothing yet," Raymond replied.

During it all, Mom remained silent. Apparently, she was good at that. She'd held on to this secret their entire lives.

It made him surly. "Ask Mom. I'm sure she knows."

"Leave her alone," Dominick growled.

"I'm sorry." Something she'd said a hundred times since the revelation. "I only ever wanted to protect you."

Even with the apology, the resentment proved hard to tamp. How could she do this to them? As kids, he could understand not burdening them, but for fuck's sake, he and a few of his siblings were in their thirties. As old as she had been when she chose to take action and save their lives.

Stefan had a harsh suggestion. "You should put our past on a backburner. It's waited this long. It can wait a little longer. We need to know more about this wolf pack." Because it was one thing to act blasé when a handful of folks posed a threat, but judging by the flow of people, this pack appeared to be numerous.

The danger level doubled.

"Well, excuse me for not giving them the same priority as you," Raymond snapped.

"Can't you see the danger they pose? Have you forgotten what they did to Dom and Anika?"

"They never actually hurt me," Anika reminded.

"Or me," Dominick added.

"They're not out to get us." Raymond's two cents.

"You need to stop being so paranoid," Mom said. "They just want to meet us."

"Or get us in one spot to take us out," Stefan couldn't help but mutter.

"Does this look like the kind of neighborhood people get killed in?" Mom swept a hand at the perfect lawns, the curtained windows, the smiling people all headed for the park.

There was a spot in the driveway of the house they were visiting. Mom parked in it, but for a second, no one moved.

"There are a lot more people than expected," Mom remarked in a low mutter.

"It's not too late to leave," Stefan suggested.

"He might have a point." Dominick took his side.

"Do you think they'd be inviting kids to a take-down? I've seen a few baby carriers. Meaning babies. Do you really think they'd do anything to put them in danger?" Anika asked.

It occurred to Stefan that some people had no

regard for life. He'd read about the deaths in the news, if they reported them. Society had gotten desensitized about violence as the media frothed over politics instead.

But his sister had a point as well. The way people were flowing up the sidewalk, heading for the path leading into a park. They had smiles and strollers. Not guns and threats.

"If you're wrong about this, I will haunt your ass," Stefan muttered, getting out of the emasculator. He instantly went tense. Something in the air tickled at him, raised the hairs on his neck—his hackles.

"Maybe we should send Anika and Mom home," he said in an aside to his brother Dominick, who'd emerged behind him. He remained too aware and none too keen on all the stares being tossed their way.

Anika snorted. "Stop being so dramatic. They're not going to murder us on the sidewalk."

Logically he knew that, and yet his gut clenched. It wanted to drop into flight mode. Danger. Danger all around.

Mom put a hand on him and whispered, "It's okay. You can walk away if needed."

How dare she show him compassion?

He shrugged her off. "I can do this. I'm fine."

"You better be, pussy," Dominick drawled.

"Fuck you," Stefan muttered.

"Boys, behave," Mom admonished. "And get moving. Your sister is already going inside."

"What?" A glance showed Maeve disappearing into the house. "Ray, with me." With quick strides, he and Raymond headed up the path, while Dominick stayed with Mom and his woman.

At the door, they were halted by a massive dude in a T-shirt that showed a scene from a Monty Python movie with the black knight. The dude at least had good taste.

Dude also had an incredible scowl. "I don't know you."

Stefan glared right back. "Doesn't matter if you do or not since we were invited."

To his surprise, the big dude broke into a smile. "Judging by the smell, you must be those pussy cats I've been hearing about. Do any of you play hockey?"

The question took him by surprise, but Dominick, who'd arrived with the ladies, latched onto it. "I used to play on the base. But it's been a few years since I strapped on skates."

"Defense or offense?"

"Goalie."

"Really?" Dude's face lit up. "We just lost ours. Job out west." With that icebreaker, Dominick, Anika, and the dude, whose name was Percy, began to chat.

Mom put her hand on his arm. "They seem like a friendly bunch."

They did. But Stefan wasn't fooled by their outward appearance. He prickled all over. "Keep your guard up."

They stepped into a middleclass home with a wide entrance that led up some stairs and had a classic layout. Living room on one side, dining room on the other and large kitchen with family room at the back.

They milled around in the front hall until a rangy fellow with a clean-shaven jaw and dark hair appeared. "If it isn't the Hubbard clan. You must be the matriarch, Nanette Hubbard. I just met your daughter. Gwayne Pendraggun." He held out a massive hand.

Mom had her hand engulfed by Gwayne's. "So you're the alpha I've heard about. These are my sons Stefan and Raymond."

The alpha's gaze tracked over them, quickly assessing, never losing that smile. "You seem to be missing a few of your clan."

"Dominick is chatting about hockey with some guy called Percy," Stefan supplied.

"That still leaves several unaccounted for." The man spoke softly, still with a smile, but they all heard the thread of steel.

"The two youngest are at home being babysat by

my daughter, Pamela. Jessie is out of town, and Daeve is wherever the military deployed him," Mom answered politely, but the question made Stefan seethe. Who the fuck was this guy to even ask?

"I see. Next time bring all the children currently in residence. We are a family-oriented pack, as you can see."

Shy Raymond was the one to blurt out, "Are you all wolves?"

Gwayne's brows rose. "That was to the point."

"But cuts through the bullshit. Are you, or aren't you?" Stefan drawled.

The cool gaze rested briefly on him. "You are here for my pack to meet and to aid in our upcoming decision about what to do about your presence in our territory."

"How about you go do your thing, and we do ours?"

"That isn't how this works. And you know that, which is why you're here."

"I thought we were here to feed your ego." Stefan couldn't help himself.

Mom hissed. "Don't be rude."

Gwayne lifted a hand. "Let him speak. I'd rather hear it now and deal with it."

The guy wanted to hear it? Stefan had no problem unloading. "I don't see why we have to kiss his ass for the right to stay here. We've been living just fine for the past twenty-some years. Now, all of a sudden, he tells us we gotta bow and scrape because he says so?"

The other man arched a brow. "With that kind of attitude, it will be hard to convince my pack you're not a threat."

"How is our little family a threat?"

It wasn't Gwayne who answered, but Nimway as she made a sudden appearance. "It's not you but the people digging into your family that are the issue."

6

Nimway meant to stay away from Stefan. Their one meeting had left her annoyed. Heated. Pacing.

What an unlikeable man. At least on the surface. She'd caught glimpses at their last meeting of another person underneath, someone seeking answers, who'd struggled alone trying to come to grips with the fact he wasn't like everyone else.

A man who'd asked for help—and been refused by her.

And I stand by that choice. She couldn't teach him. As a matter of fact, she should stay far away to avoid the odd allure Stefan had about him. She couldn't pinpoint what made him so irresistible.

The red hair? Definitely sexy.

The beard? She wanted to stroke it.

That body... Well, she could have some fun with that firm bod of his.

But she wouldn't because a good pack member didn't sleep with the enemy. A beta didn't get too close to a guy who could be a danger to her pack. Her family.

Stefan appeared determined to ignore the fact they'd do anything to keep their secrets. Killing? Happened more often than people knew. Nimway was the one who coordinated the mishaps.

Death was a part of life. Cold, yet necessary. The things she did to protect her family couldn't have emotion attached to them. Which was why she couldn't afford to like Stefan. He might have to die.

His whole family might.

Already she was calculating the ways she could act. Imagining ice flowing in her veins. Or so she told herself as she gravitated toward Stefan the moment he arrived at her brother's house. Her home, too, since the tragedy that befell her brother. Gwayne had not yet recovered from losing his wife and child in one swoop. Despite his choosing to sleep in the cold, dark room in the basement, she heard him yelling when the nightmares hit.

Would Stefan wake in a cold sweat if he lost someone in his family? For some reason the thought of upsetting him bothered. Maybe there was a better solution?

Speaking of whom, he glared at her. He didn't like the fact she knew something he didn't.

"What do you mean someone is digging into my family's business?"

"Do you have a problem understanding words?" she mocked. "Someone has taken an interest in the Hubbards. And by the way, your farm is being watched."

His mouth worked, and before he could reply, his brother stepped in. "How would you know if anyone was watching us? Or looking into us for that matter?"

Gwayne snorted. "Are you that oblivious? The moment we heard the report of a big cat attacking someone in the city, we went looking and found you easily. The victim's ex-wife is dating your brother, Dominick."

"How far have you dug into our family?" Stefan asked.

"Not far enough yet. And more worrisome, none of you noticed." Gwayne was the one to rumble in rebuke. "Haven't you instituted any kind of protection for your family?"

Raymond was the one to shift and grimace. "Until recently, I had no idea we had anything to hide."

"Jeezus." She raked fingers through her hair. "I can't believe you haven't noticed the drive-bys in front of your place, not to mention the people we've had stationed watching."

"What are you talking about?" Raymond frowned. "I have a camera at the entrance to the driveway. I never saw anything."

His indignation made her laugh. "Oh sweetie, they are not amateurs. They'll have used disruptors. Watch the video feed again and you'll notice a stutter in the footage."

"I saw it and assumed it was a malfunction. I had a new camera ordered, but it's taking a few days to arrive." Raymond's chin hung even lower.

"Wouldn't make a difference."

"Fuck me." Stefan tugged his beard.

She wanted to tug his beard. She stuck to the problem at hand. "You're under surveillance, and not just by us. We've had our people keeping an eye on your family. Your online records have been accessed within the last forty-eight hours. You might want to watch for drones and don't let anyone inside in case they're trying to plant bugs."

Stefan's entire family gaped at her, including the old lady. It baffled her that the pack had had only just now stumbled across them. They were completely clueless about protecting themselves. A different person might have felt sympathy; however, she wasn't in a position where she could afford to be soft.

"Your property is large, and that massive open space around the house is most likely making it harder for them to sneak a peek without you noticing. But you'll need to add some precautions to curtail any incursions. We have a plan for the watchers to draw their attention elsewhere, but your family needs to do something about your online presence. Your brother Tyson is especially fond of videos."

"I've scrubbed the worst ones the moment they're flagged," Raymond mumbled.

"But not before they were seen in some cases," Nimway pointed out.

"Sloppy," Gwayne growled. "The number one rule is don't draw attention. It endangers us all."

Stefan smirked. "All the more reason for each of us to go our separate ways."

"Don't be so hasty." Her brother smiled, a predator about to pounce its prey.

Only Stefan wasn't a coward. He stood tall in front of Gwayne.

Which was when the little old lady finally shoved her way between them. "Shut down the testosterone, boys. There are ladies present."

Nimway glanced around. Since when?

Stefan laughed. "You've obviously not met Nimway."

For some reason his supposed insult brought a

smile. "I'm flattered to know you've been thinking about me since we met, baby." Nimway winked.

Rather than flare his anger, he flirted back. "I've been waiting for his moment, darling." Crooned soft and sexy. It brought heat to her cheeks, especially since her brother eyed her with curiosity.

"Well, hello there, Nimway. I'm Nannette Hubbard. These nitwits' mom." The eldest Hubbard held out her hand. Her grip proved firm and strong.

Nimway cocked her head. "Nimway Pendraggun. Pack beta."

"Second in command?" Elder Hubbard's expression brightened.

"Nepotism is alive and well," Stefan drawled, eying Gwayne.

"Actually," Nimway snapped, "positions in the pack are decided by competence and not what dangles between the legs."

"Is that what you tell yourself to feel better?"

He deserved the slug to his gut that folded him over. And she was gratified that his mother grabbed him by the ear and hissed, "That was unacceptable. Apologize this instant."

Her brother leaned close and whispered, "I like the old lady."

So did she. Maybe she could find a way to spare her life.

Stefan obviously loved his mom, too, because,

sullen faced, he mumbled, "Sorry. That was a shitty thing to say."

His mother jabbed him. "Now say it like you mean it."

His lips twisted. and his tone was wry. "It was an asshole thing to say, but at the same time, I'd do it again. Because you're annoying."

"It's called assertive. You should try coming out of your cave and seeing the modern world sometime," she sassed.

"Don't knock my warm and cozy cave until you try it." A purred suggestion, probably meant to throw her off balance.

As if she were an amateur. "I'll bring the champagne."

"Um, guys, Mom is right there," Raymond whispered loudly.

"Let the children flirt."

Elder Hubbard smiled, the pleased grin of a matchmaker. Nimway had seen it before.

So had Stefan, apparently. "We aren't flirting."

"Never." Nimway would keep her distance.

A shout drew their attention. *"Fucker, I saw you touch her ass."*

"I was aiming for yours," taunted the replying person.

Crash.

Gwayne frowned. "I better go crack some heads together. Nim, take care of our guests."

"Because I'm a fucking hostess," she grumbled as her brother strode away. At least she wasn't alone with Stefan.

"So tell me, Nimway, are you single?" Elder Hubbard asked.

"Excuse me?" She blinked at the older lady.

"A smart girl like you. I mean to attain your position, you probably had to work twice as hard as a male. Plus, I'll bet you had to prove you were the best and not just the boss's sister." Elder Hubbard beamed.

"I guess," she mumbled. What the old lady said was true. She'd had to work her ass off to show the pack she deserved it more than anyone else.

"What a fine example you are. I'd love for you to meet my daughters."

"Er, what?" Stefan appeared as surprised as she felt.

"It's important for young women to meet other women who've achieved success through dedication and a good work ethic. You'll make someone very lucky, won't she, boys?" Nanette Hubbard said, flipping her gaze between her two sons.

"Mom, this is not the time." Stefan groaned.

"It's never time according to you. You're getting

old, Stefan. And I'm not getting any younger. I need grandbabies," Elder Hubbard snapped.

"I'm sure Dominick is working on that with Anika."

To which Raymond muttered, "Thank fuck they were banned from the house. I swear if I caught them in the kitchen one more time..."

"Raymond!" Elder Hubbard huffed.

"What? It's true. I'm sure Dominick will have Anika knocked up in no time, and then you can change all kinds of shitty diapers and leave the rest of us alone," Raymond stated.

"Being a parent is a blessed thing," Elder Hubbard insisted.

"If you say so," was Nimway's hushed reply.

Stefan glanced at her and grinned. It brought out a dimple in his cheek. Dear God, she was pretty sure an ovary hiccupped.

"Since you two seem to be getting along so well, Raymond and I will go check out the buffet table. I think I saw those little crustless sandwiches he likes."

"Really?" Raymond's gaze tilted, and once he caught sight of the food table, the man practically dragged his mother toward it.

Nimway arched a brow. "Not subtle, is she?"

"Gee, did you notice? At least she left. Five more

minutes and she'd have planned our engagement and named our children."

"You and me, married?" She laughed. Hard.

He didn't appear as amused as her. "Are you done?"

"Depends. You going to make another joke?"

"No because you might hit me again."

"You deserved it. That wasn't a joke."

He sighed. "No, it wasn't. I was being intentionally mean."

"Why?"

"Because I don't want to like you."

Well, that was unexpected. Both his reply and, judging by his face, the fact he'd not meant to admit it. They stared at each other, the moment awkward.

She shuffled first. "Don't worry, baby, even if you were in love, it would never work because I can't stand the stench of you."

His jaw tightened. "You'll have to deal with it a bit longer because I want to talk to you about spying on my family." Raucous laughter brought a crease to his brow. "Can we talk somewhere a little quieter?"

"Not right now we can't." Nimway shook her head. "The barbecue is coming out as we speak, and I am not missing out on the best meal of the year."

"What are you wearing?" he asked, as he finally appeared to notice her shirt.

"Don't tell me this wasn't your favorite cereal growing up." She stuck out her tits to show off the cartoon stretched across, lots of orange and blue. The frosted crunchy stuff was a must-have in her home.

"It's processed crap. My mom usually fed us pancakes or French toast, eggs, and sausage."

"Mmm, that does sound good. Can you cook?" She couldn't have said why she asked.

"No."

Probably a good thing. She didn't need him to become even more appealing.

She led the way to the backyard, and he stuck close to her side. "I'd say someone stalking my family is more important than food."

She cast him a glance. "It is, which is why it's being handled."

"By who?"

"Who do you think?" she drawled.

"Your brother?"

Sexist ass!

She hip-checked him and sent him careening.

7

Nimway stalked off. It took a moment before Stefan caught up to her. "Why are you pissed again?"

"You seem to think because I'm a woman I can't do shit." An attitude she'd been fighting her entire life.

"Well, excuse me. It's not like you said, hey, I'm in charge of security. Or whatever it is you do."

She grabbed a disposable plastic plate. It would be washed and given to Herb, who'd melt it and use it with his 3D printer to make simple stuff for the pack.

"I'm pack beta. That means second in command, in charge of keeping the pack safe whether from outside or inside forces."

"How?" he asked, shuffling with her in the line

heading for the many barbecues set up on the stone patio. Some powered by propane but a few by the more aromatic charcoal.

"How do we prevent someone from telling the world our secret?" She held out her plate for a steak. "We make sure no one talks."

"You threaten them?"

As she headed for the rib station, she shrugged. "Sometimes."

He went silent, and she got the impression he finally understood how serious the pack took threats.

They loaded up some plates, because one just didn't have enough room to do justice to the many side dishes. There were many varieties of salads, and not just the crisp vegetable kind but also creamy potato and pasta. Balancing two heavy plates, she led the way out of the backyard into the park that formed a courtyard of sorts for the houses surrounding it. All around, the homes had barbecues going, voices raised, and lights strung. There were no fences here.

He glanced around before noting. "Every single place around this park belongs to your pack."

"Yup. Safety in numbers."

"You'd think it would draw more notice."

"We protect each other."

"And fuck outsiders."

"Pretty much," she agreed.

She chose a spot under a spreading oak, sitting cross-legged on the ground and balancing her plates in her lap.

He sank close by, and they ate for a bit in silence until he groaned and said, "Don't tell my mom, but these ribs are delicious."

She smiled through sauced and greasy lips. "Told you so."

They worked their way through the food, until she wished she'd worn leggings instead of jeans. Would he notice if she unsnapped the button?

She was just about to try and give herself some room to bloat when Charlene ran up. She was five years old and cute as a button, huffing as she exclaimed, "They're bringing up the pig."

"The what?"

"You'll see."

The slow-roasted pig proved succulent. And delicious.

Despite being full, they ate some more. He flicked his belt looser, and since he went first, it was fine now for her to pop a button.

Sated, she stopped eyeballing food to focus more on the party.

She wasn't technically doing security for the event. The pack had a team on duty, keeping an eye. Outsiders wouldn't be allowed into the neighborhood tonight except for the Hubbards, who'd been invited. A test run of sorts to see if they could get a feel for the family before rendering a final decision on their fate.

To their credit, Nimway noticed how the Hubbard people seemed to have no problem blending in with the pack. Nanette had parked herself with the other matriarchs and, by their faces and laughter, exchanged stories. Raymond, the less-seen brother, had found the one table with the nerd crew. Those rebels sat parked on their asses, their faces illuminated by screens. The others in his family were mingling and smiling and flirting.

All in all, a party going well, and yet Stefan appeared suspicious.

"What's wrong?" she asked as she led him to the dessert table. They had to fill their plates again before they wandered off to eat their prize.

"It occurs to me that the kindness we're seeing here is contrary to the way your brother initially approached us." He spoke of their confrontation with Dominick, when they'd kidnapped his girlfriend.

Not their finest plan. In her defense, they'd had to move fast once they realized someone might be drawing attention to their territory.

"At the time, we had no idea if you posed a threat or not."

His lips twisted. "I take it, since we're in the

heart of your neighborhood, we've been deemed harmless."

"Not exactly."

"Meaning what?"

"That the pack will soon decide on your fate."

"The pack or your brother?"

"They usually follow the will of the alpha."

"And as his number two, does that make you his enforcer?"

"If needed." She didn't see a point in lying.

Rather than recoil, he actually tried to poke at her conscience. "And you're okay with murdering people because he asks you to?"

"The pack is everything." She'd learned long ago to wall away any sympathy when it came to the safety of her people.

"Implying you'd kill my family if you thought them a threat."

"I would."

"But now that we're getting along, does this mean we've passed your test?"

"Do you really care?"

He leaned against the wall on the side of the house where they'd gone for some privacy. "I was doing just fine before you all came along, and I'll still be okay if you're not around, too."

For some reason that stung. "If you believe that, then why did you even bother coming?"

"To ensure my family's safety."

"Is that all?" Had he truly only come for one reason?

"No." He ducked his head. And whispered, "I know I shouldn't. But I want…"

For a second her lips parted. *Want? Yes, I want—*

"I need answers."

His statement snapped her reverie. "I don't think so."

"I haven't even asked any yet," he exclaimed.

"Doesn't matter. The last time we spoke, you argued with everything I said."

"Did not."

A rude sound erupted from her. "He says even as he's doing it again."

"Can you blame me for questioning what you say? Can you grasp the fact it's hard to accept that you, morphing, werewolves, and packs, all of it is real?"

"How can it be hard? You've experienced it."

"I thought I was a freak of nature. One in a million." At least he didn't deny it anymore.

"Oh, you're still rare, baby. Just not as rare as you thought."

He slewed an angry gaze at her. "Not funny. I would have never wished this on my family."

"Stop acting as if it's a curse or an illness."

"Isn't lycanthropy a virus?"

That brought a chuckle to her lips. "Stop getting your knowledge from movies and television. I'm here to tell you, right now, that werewolves are born. Would you like me to arrange for you to watch the next birth?"

He paled. "No thanks."

"We don't come out hairy or with teeth by the way. That usually only starts around the six-month mark."

"You turn into wolves that young?"

She frowned. "You sound surprised."

"Because I was a teenager my first time."

Her mouth rounded. "That old?"

He winced. "I take it that's unusual."

"Almost unheard of. A side effect perhaps of whatever was done to you." Which she had to admit she was curious about. "Do you remember anything at all from your time in captivity? Did all of you come from the same place? The birth records I've seen all show you being three years old when you were adopted, except for Dominick and Jessie. They were both slightly older."

"How do you know so much about my family?"

"It's my job."

"You're good," he muttered. "Too good. But it won't do any good. I tried looking into our past. I found nothing."

"That's because you don't have our resources. What about memories?"

He shook his head. "I can't remember shit."

"You've tried?"

"Well, yeah, but nothing really concrete."

"Even under hypnosis?" Nimway asked.

He blinked at her. "Like fuck."

"It might help you recall the early years." She couldn't help but prod.

"Maybe I don't want to."

"Don't you want to know where you came from?"

"Not really. Those who made us are sick, murdering bastards."

"Which is why it's important we figure out who they are, and if they're the ones currently investigating your family."

He turned pale. "What a clusterfuck." He pulled out a cigarette, but before he lit it, she knocked his hand away.

"No smoking. There are kids around."

"In the yard."

"No. Smoking." She grabbed his hand and shredded the cigarette.

"When agitated, I either smoke or fuck. Choose."

"We could get a beer."

"I don't drink." Flatly spoken.

She'd noticed him getting juice but hadn't clued in he'd remained dry. "You shouldn't smoke."

"My body, my choice."

"You're an ass."

"I'm being as annoying as you," he stated. "Giving me half answers about everything. Telling me my family is in danger and then no other information, making it harder for me to protect them."

"Don't worry about them. They're safe for the moment. We planted something for the watchers to follow. They took the bait and are on a wild chase, but they might be back."

"What bait?"

"A few rumors in an online social media group of a large animal stalking people in a neighborhood on the opposite side of the city. Possibly a cat."

"You planted a rumor?" He had an incredulous note in his query.

"And it worked. When possible, try to throw off suspicion by laying a false trail. If they give up, it's the best-case scenario."

"You're really thought about this shit."

"We've had to in order to survive."

"What do you fear?" he asked.

"As if you don't know."

His chin dropped. "Discovery."

8

ADMITTING HIS BIGGEST FEAR LIBERATED
Stefan, even as it left him vulnerable.

She put a hand over his. "Preventing discovery is
my job. It helps with the anxiety about it."

"Really? Because it would be nice to not be suspicious that I'm being watched all the time."

"Oh, you should still suspect everyone and everything." Her grin shone with mischief.

"Even you?" His query low and husky.

"Especially me." Again with the lilt in her words.
Was she flirting?

"Am I supposed to believe this is flying under the
radar?" he asked. He waved a hand toward the lit
end of the alley between the houses, filled with
strung patio lanterns, music, and the hum of voices.
"This seems like you're asking to be found out."

"It's called hiding in plain sight. When you look around, what do you see?"

"A lot of werewolves."

"Where? Show me one."

He opened and shut his mouth. "Well, none at the moment."

"And you'll never see one here. It's one of our most enforced rules."

"You banned morphing."

"Only inside the city. Wolves don't belong in suburbia. Anyone who wants to run on four legs has to go somewhere a wolf wouldn't be out of place."

"Meaning you head out of the valley for some stretches of forest."

"Some do go that far. Those of us who need to stretch more often can get away with running along the Trans Canada Trail. Just park on Westridge and head in, looking like you're going for a jog. Slip into the woods, strip, and boom." She snapped her fingers. "You can get a few hours in."

"What if you're seen?"

"So long as we're not menacing, people can call in wolf sightings. Our guy who processes the calls will label it a coyote. Dangerous to household pets. Not humans."

"What if someone thinks you are a danger and does something?"

She arched a brow. "We live in Ottawa, Canada.

No shooting animals unless you have a tag from the government."

"Not everyone obeys the law."

She rolled her eyes. "Not everyone goes jogging on a nature trail armed to kill wolves. As a matter of fact, I'd go so far as to call it rare if it ever happens."

He wanted to be contrary and ague some more, only to realize he was doing it to her again. She was giving him answers, and he was arguing.

Fuck me, I am annoying. He needed to stop being a dick. "How often do you go furry?"

She rolled her shoulders. "Not as often as I'd like. Most of my work happens in the city."

"Wouldn't it make more sense for you all to live in the country so you didn't have to hide?"

"And commute how long to work each day?" She arched a brow. "You do realize the bills have to be paid. A wolf's gotta have meat in the fridge."

"This is crazy." He pulled another cigarette, only to have Nimway knock it away. Again.

"Jeezus, it's just a smoke." He defiantly pulled a third.

She leaned in and yanked it, squishing it to tobacco dust. She moved close enough to whisper on his lips, "Smoking is gross."

"You're allowed to think that. I happen to like it, and I told you, when I get fucked up, I need to screw, or I smoke." Once upon a time, he'd done harder shit. He wouldn't lose that kind of control again.

"No. Smoking." The words fluttered against his mouth.

So close. Her scent, sweet and musky all at once, swirled around him. Surely, she knew how she tempted. It wouldn't take much movement on his part to kiss her.

He fought against the urge.

"What's wrong, baby? You're awfully quiet all of a sudden."

"Just thinking about everything you've told me."

"Is that all, *baby?*" The last word teased him.

"What are you doing?" he asked. Other than driving him wild.

"Trying to make you kiss me. But since you're being a fucking gentleman—" She kissed him.

For a moment, surprise held Stefan still, and then he opened his mouth and his tongue welcomed her in.

Sensual heat. Desire. A throbbing need filled him.

He lost track of time and place. He was on fire. Every stroke of her tongue and grind of her pelvis stoked the heat.

She groped him, cupping his ass through his jeans. Sliding her hands into the snug fabric and digging her nails in. He would have done the same if they'd not been interrupted.

"Eeew. They're kissing." The bucket of cold water came in the form of the same little girl as before.

"It is nasty, I agree." The voice of Gwayne, Nimway's brother.

Fuck.

She practically leaped out of his arms as she exclaimed, "Gwayne, um, did you need something?"

"Am I interrupting?" Gwayne's voice was much too smooth. The violent glitter in his eyes didn't bode well.

Not that Stefan could blame him. He'd have done the same if he'd caught his sister kissing the enemy.

"What do you want?" Nimway snapped.

It was the little girl who pointed at Stefan. "Need you. Big kitty is guarding the dessert table." Adorably lisped, which was probably why it didn't make sense.

"I don't understand," Stefan said with a frown.

"Raymond." The only word Gwayne uttered before pivoting and marching off.

What about his brother Raymond? It was enough for Stefan to follow, emerging into a yard where voices buzzed and music still played, but everyone appeared riveted by something ahead of him.

As the crowd parted for Gwayne and Stefan, he finally saw what had everyone's attention. A lynx growled at anyone who came near the chocolate fountain. That wasn't the only issue.

94

Anika had her arms and legs wrapped around Dominick and appeared to be talking frantically at him, but it was only as Stefan neared the dessert table and smelled it that he understood.

Anger overflowed. He whirled on Gwayne. "What the fuck? You think it's funny to spike the chocolate with catnip? What kind of shit trick is that?"

The guy looked confused. "I swear we didn't."

"Mostly because no one would ever ruin chocolate like that," Nimway muttered, moving past him, only to freeze as the big lynx took a swipe at her.

She growled.

The cat snarled and crouched.

Fuck me.

"Raymond, no!" Stefan grabbed Nimway and tossed her behind him and then turned to face his brother, who was more susceptible to catnip than he'd led on. He must have gone for the chocolate the moment they brought it out. He always did have a sweet tooth, as did Dominick, who had to be led away, his control sorely tested.

As for Stefan? It smelled good. He'd love a bite. But one bite would lead to him waking up in the woods naked with sore and sticky parts he didn't want to think about.

He held out a hand to the lynx. "Raymond. It's me, your brother."

The cat growled.

"Don't you fucking pull that shit with me." Stefan took a step forward. "You need to come away from that fountain, buddy. It's got catnip in it."

The feline rolled its head.

"Yeah, I know it smells delicious, which is why you gotta walk away from it."

"Rawr." The cat lifted a lip, and to his surprise, Stefan snarled right back. A little more beast than he would have thought himself capable of.

The lynx blinked. And the voices around them went from excited murmurs to nothing at all.

Double fuck.

"Get out of the way," he heard his mom bark, and he turned to see her arriving with a platter of crustless sandwiches. Peanut butter and jelly. Raymond's favorite. "Come on Ray-ray. Look what Mama's got." She waggled the tray, and the cat appeared torn. Fountain or Mommy with treats?

"Ray-ray, who's my good boy?" Mom crooned.

The lynx snapped and bared teeth as he headed for Mom and her goodies. Crisis averted.

For the moment, but he had a feeling the true disaster had yet to come.

9

GWAYNE DIDN'T LET ON HOW PISSED HE WAS until the Hubbard family left. The moment they'd been confirmed gone from the neighborhood, with a tail that would watch them overnight, her brother howled, "Who the fuck spiked the food?"

Silence.

"Who was so stupid as to endanger us *all*?" The query ended on a low trebling note.

No one came forward.

That brought a deep rumble from Gwayne. "Someone saw something. Speak now or—"

A little boy raised a hand. "I know what happened, alpha."

"Bertrand?" Spoken with surprise.

The boy hung his head. "It was me. I put the spices in the chocolate."

The admission stunned. Gwayne's voice softened. "What kind of spices, Bertrand? Where did you get them?"

The boy hung his head. "I dunno."

An obvious lie.

Everyone knew it, which was why Gwayne had to deal with it publicly. "Who. Gave. It. To. You."

There was command in those words. An order from the alpha that had to be obeyed.

"Jojo." The name whispered past Bertrand's lips then in a more hyper rush, "I did it to be nice. Jojo said our guests would love it. Said it would make them so happy."

Jojo was a member of the pack who was already on probation for being a lazy shit. And now a traitor.

"Where is he?" Gwayne asked. No need to mention who.

People all around shuffled and looked. Jojo hadn't been at the barbeque. No one recalled seeing him.

A search of his place showed things missing, personal effects. His phone was on the bed.

As if that were the only way of tracking the traitor. It didn't matter how far Jojo ran. He'd put the pack in danger. He'd have to pay the price.

The party scattered from the park to the other houses, leaving Nimway alone with her brother. He stalked through his yard to the house and headed for the liquor cabinet. It brought a chill of remembrance to her skin.

Of him drunk. Depressed.

At least it didn't happen often now. After his wife and baby died—complications with the birth—he'd turned to alcohol to numb the pain. It only seemed to make it worse. He suffered way too much and emerged on the other side of his grief changed. Tougher and, yet at the same time, softer. She could tell because rather than get rid of the Hubbards before they could expose the pack, he was contemplating bringing them into their midst.

As if cats and dogs could work together.

He handed her a glass, and she grabbed it. A good thing, too, because she needed a fortifying swig when he said, "Care to explain why I caught you dry humping the red-headed one?"

She spewed the liquor.

Just her luck Gwayne was the one to interrupt one of the most heated make-out sessions of her life.

"Now that's a waste of good booze." Gwayne tossed his back.

"I don't see what the problem is," she mumbled.

"You. Him. I'm thinking either too much beer or pot. Maybe both?"

"I'm not… I mean I wasn't wasted."

"Then what possessed you?" Gwayne's dry reply.

She grimaced. "Can we leave it at bad choices?"

"That's more than a bad choice. Stefan is a possible threat to our pack, and you had your tongue down his throat."

"You're being a patriarchal ass. I'm a grown woman who can fuck whoever she likes."

"Then why not fuck someone who will actually be useful?" her brother snapped. "For years now, I've been telling you to settle down with someone. Have a kid or two to carry on our line." Because Gwayne had vowed to never remarry after his wife and child died. "And instead of choosing someone with the right kind of bloodline, you were making out with a fucking lab experiment."

"Again, I will remind you that we are in the twenty-first century and you don't have a say in who I fuck or date." As if she'd cave to his macho bullshit.

"Wrong. I do have a say, because you're beta for this pack. The one who will lead if I fall." He softened. "And you are the only family I have left. Who will carry our name after you?"

She sighed. Wanted to tell him it was time he got over his grief. But at the same time, he'd suffered so much when they died.

"I'm sorry, Gwayne, but I'm not going to tie myself to someone just because they're pack. On the contrary, you should be cautioning us against it. For God's sake, you've read the reports on inbreeding."

"We've been careful."

Yeah, limiting who could date who. They'd long ago banned first cousins. "So careful that our birth rate is lower than ever because our gene pool is too small."

"What do you suggest then?" Gwayne snapped, the argument a familiar one. "You know mixing with humans doesn't always result in a lycan."

"Never said humans. What about another type of shifter?" She couldn't have said why she threw it out there, and yet she pictured a certain pompous bearded ginger.

"Wait, are you telling me you actually planned to bed Stefan?"

"Yes." It had nothing to do with carrying on the family name, but more because he set her panties on fire.

"Think he'd still be willing after what happened tonight?"

"No!" Was her brother nuts? Now that the blood was back in her brain, she could see getting involved would end badly.

"Yeah, Stefan seemed pretty pissy." Gwayne rubbed his chin. "What about the other brother?"

"Raymond?" she squeaked. "What about him?"

"He seems the decent sort."

"For what?"

"An alliance between our families."

She shook her head violently. "Like fuck."

"Think of it for a second. It solves so many problems at once." Gwayne began pacing with enthusiasm, and she got worried.

"You are not pimping me out."

"Yet you're the one who suggested it." His voice lowered dangerously. "It would make a perfect solution, given your concerns about inbreeding. Think of it. We form an alliance with a smaller pack while, at the same time, introducing new bloodlines into our gene pool to meet your picky demands."

"It's not picky." She just didn't want to date guys who felt like brothers. Gross.

"Says the girl who left me no choice."

She could have been a cunt and yelled a choice at him. Told him to stop putting his ex-wife on a pedestal. She'd been far from perfect. But she couldn't malign a dead woman. "Arranged marriages are archaic."

"I know you'll do what's right for the pack."

"Don't you dare say this is for the pack!"

"As your alpha, I command you to—" Before Gwayne spilled his misogynistic bright idea, she slugged him.

10

Stefan's phone rang at an ungodly hour. He knew this because he was still asleep in bed. He would have ignored it but for the fact the ringtone belonged to the most important person in the world.

"This better be important, Mom," he said.

"The wolves are demanding an alliance," she said.

He blinked at the clock. "Now? It's six a.m."

"And well past time you got up."

"I didn't get home until after two." Because that was how long it took to calm Ray down. Apparently, seeing his brothers turn into cats hadn't prepared the guy for his own transformation. It didn't help it was in public and Ray had the humiliating video from his new hacker friends to prove it.

Although Stefan did chuckle at the meme that showed a mash-up of an image of Ray intent over his laptop with that of the cat guarding the chocolate fountain with the caption, *Don't mess with my machine, or I will eat your face.*

"You could have spent the night at home," his mother chided.

Because a grown man wanted to sleep in a bunkbed with his brothers. No thanks.

Not to mention, he couldn't go home because then he'd be tempted by the fucking plant in his brother's basement lair. He knew there was catnip down there. He'd seen it. Smelled it. How Ray had held out, he didn't know, because Stefan wanted it with a hunger that had him pulling out a cigarette even now. Only he didn't light it.

Nimway really hated smoking. Even kissed him to prove it.

What would have happened if they'd not been interrupted?

"Stefan? Are you there? Did you go back to sleep?"

He wished. He lit the smoke and exhaled an acrid puff. "I'm awake, and you need to start over. From the beginning this time."

"Gwayne called me last night."

"Gwayne is it now?" he drawled, taking another

puff. Dry smoke first thing in the morning without a coffee? Not the tastiest thing.

"He's a good man. You should give him a chance."

He swung his legs over the edge of his bed. "I did, by going to that fucking barbecue, and you know what happened? My brother got drugged."

"It wasn't Gwayne's fault."

Stefan snorted. "His party. His people. They had to know it was spiked." Done on purpose hoping one of them would take the bait and shift. To what end he didn't know.

"Gwayne told me only he and a trusted few knew about the catnip. They found a package with the herb, much like the one Dominick received, in the perpetrator's house."

"They know who did it?"

"Yes. And they are looking for him."

"You seem well informed."

"I had a long talk with Gwayne. He's a nice boy. Lost his parents when he was eighteen. Car crash. Both at once."

Meaning Nimway was an orphan.

"Did you know he and his siblings are all named after King Arthur characters?"

"Why?"

"Why not?" Mom sassed.

"Is there any reason I should care other than the fact you're now Gwayne's best friend?"

"I thought it was nice he called to apologize. He wants to ensure it never happens again."

He lit another cigarette after the one in his hand burned down. Suck. Blow. "And exactly how are they going to stop their people from exposing us?" Because too many of them knew their weakness. Their kryptonite.

"We join the pack."

Laughter burst out of him. He couldn't help it. "Please. As if they'd even let us."

"They will and I don't see any other choice."

He sucked a few drags before croaking, "Why, Mom? How does that help us? We've been doing fine until now."

"That was before. With what we know now about you and your brothers, possibly all of you…" Mom's voice softened. "I know you don't like it. But as things change, we must change too."

"Don't you spout that Zen crap before my first cup of coffee," he grumbled, finally managing to shuffle from bed to kitchen.

"It's common sense. Only someone who wants to fail doesn't know how to adapt and swing with the punches."

"Can we stop with the metaphors?" Cigarette in one hand, phone sitting on the counter, speaker enabled, he put in a k-cup and waited for his coffee to brew. The longest thirty seconds ever.

"Fine, you want to change the subject, then let's talk about Gwayne's sister."

He stiffened as he pulled his mug free and headed for the honey. "What about her?"

"You spent an awful lot of time with her."

In retrospect, he had spent the entire fucking time with her, which was unusual for Stefan. "She's interesting." True, and it admitted too much.

His mother went quiet. "I hear her mouth was very interesting last night."

"Mom!"

"Do you know how embarrassing it is to have someone mention her son couldn't keep it in his pants for one day!" she yelled right back.

"It didn't go that far."

"But you did seduce her. Which explains why Gwayne was asking about your intentions."

Saying "get laid" would probably get him in trouble. "My intentions? Jeezus, Mom. It was a kiss. Nothing more."

"That's kind of callous. I'm surprised by you."

"Since when? We all know I'm the whore in the family." The moment he said it he closed his eyes.

It got quiet.

Then his mother said, "That's a filthy word. Nothing wrong with sex between consenting adults."

A complete about-turn given her harangue about the kiss.

"We are not discussing this, Mom."

"I love you no matter what, Stefan."

"I love you, too." Had from the day she'd given him a shiny red apple and a chance to decide who he'd become. Not her fault he'd failed along the way.

"Why is she interesting, this girl?"

"I don't know. Because she is." And it was also impossible. Wolf. Tiger. Totally wrong for each other, and yet their lips fit perfectly.

"Last night I was talking to a few of the more mature people in the pack. They told me Nimway could have been alpha if she wanted, only she didn't want to fight her brother."

"Because fighting is a brilliant way to choose a leader."

"Would you feel better if I said that the battle includes a knowledge portion?"

Unbidden, his lip quirked. "A test? I can see why she wouldn't want to do it."

"All this to say, she's not someone you should be fucking around with." Mom expelled a rare expletive.

"I'm well aware." He already knew she held rank by the way people deferred to her. She was assertive. Controlling. Sexy as fuck.

"Are you? Because, while you were busy making googly eyes with her, some of us were gathering intel. Did you know they rule in threes? Alpha, beta, and the omega, who is an older member considered the wisest in the pack. In this case, Magda, no relation to Gwayne or Nimway, seventy-nine but looking forty. Those three set policy and handle the running of the group. To enforce the laws of the pack, they have quints."

"What the fuck is that?" The strange word made no sense to him.

"What you'd call protective units. At any given time, there is at least one quint on duty. Five people on shift for eight hours, guarding the neighborhood. Two on foot patrol. Another pair stationary on the outskirts of their residential zone. And then, in an unknown location, a fifth person acting as the hub."

"You learned this with the old ladies?"

"Expect a cuff for that next time I see you," Mom snapped.

There wasn't enough caffeine in the world to deal with his mom's regurgitation of information this morning. "It is too fucking early for this, Mom."

"Too bad. We need to be informed, or are you somehow completely oblivious to the fact we can't ask normal people for help?"

"Help with what?"

"You're being stubborn for the sake of being stubborn."

He was. Blame the hot girl. He made another cup

of coffee. He really should invest in an espresso machine for the bigger caffeine jolt.

"Yeah, I'm being stubborn because I am not ready to accept these strangers as our saviors. Excuse me for being a little suspicious."

"Suspicious should have been you in the face of that odd-colored macaroni salad. And don't deny the huge spoonful you scooped. I can't believe you managed to fill two plates from that merely adequate spread." Mom sniffed.

"Excuse me. While you were learning new words, I was finding out about the people watching us."

"And? What did you learn?"

That Nimway was sexier than ever.

11

No way would Stefan admit to his mom he liked Nimway. However, he couldn't say nothing.

"I learned that Tyson needs his social media taken away."

"Why? What has he done?"

"More like what hasn't he. Tyson's been indiscreet." He threw his brother under the bus rather than admit he'd just talked with Nimway. About food. Listening to her concise and sarcastic remarks about people at the party—all of whom she knew.

The biggest family he could have imagined. For as long as he could remember, it had only ever been the kids and Mom. No aunts, uncles, grandparents, or cousins. No one but themselves. The wolf pack might not be related by blood, but they'd chosen to be tight knit for another reason. Just like the Hubbard family.

"Do you really believe all those people we saw last night can shift?" Which sounded less alien than morph. And anything sounded better than huani-morph, a stupid phrase coined by Mom's brother, Johan Philips. Their creator coined it to signify a human to animal morph. He should have run it by a PR department first.

"I think that enough of them actually do that it would be beneficial for the family to pursue ties with them. After all, wouldn't it be nice to date someone that knows your secret?" Mom slyly suggested.

It did tempt a little. Imagine no fear of discovery. Had that been what held him back from true intimacy this entire time? A terror that someone would discover his secret and sell him out? That he would be rejected once more. The little boy who'd been cast aside because he wasn't good enough.

Never mind the fact he had a better life with Mom. *Knowing you're flawed hurts.*

"Assuming they'd date us. We're not like them," he reminded his mom.

"You both change shapes."

She reduced it to a very generic denominator. "Even if we ignore the opposite species thing, you're forgetting the fact that, while we were made, the people in that pack were born that way."

"And so will your children."

The very idea froze the blood in his veins. "I'm not having kids." Not passing on this strange affliction.

"You say that now, but when you meet the right person, you'll change your mind."

His mind flashed to Nimway and then stalled. "No. I'll never be ready for that level of commitment. Hell, why do you think I've held off on getting a pet?" Although it should be noted he'd enjoyed petting Nim.

"You're so cute when you're wrong. One day, you'll remember saying that and laugh."

"I'm not ever getting married, Mom."

"If you say so." His mom sang it.

He hated it when she did that. "Are you done shitting on my morning because I think I need a very greasy, high-carb breakfast. From a diner."

Rather than rail about his choices in food, his mom got quiet then said, "Enjoy your breakfast. I'll call your brothers and let them know the news."

"What news?"

"The other reason for Gwayne's call. The Valley Pack is willing to accept us into their group."

"They are?" Then he added a more suspicious. "What are they demanding in return?"

"A pledge of fealty."

He snorted. "I am not bending a knee just cause

some hairball has shown up in our lives with delusions of ruling the city."

"Not a delusion. You saw all the people at the party. We're just peanuts compared to them."

The reminder creased his brow. The pack outnumbered his family, and should they decide to oust them...people would get hurt. People he loved.

"I don't understand why they can't just let us live quietly."

"You know why. Because we were indiscreet. It's time to admit we don't know what we're doing, Stefan. We are in over our heads." Her tone softened as she added, "I can't afford for us to be hasty and reject them outright. Keep in mind it's not the older kids we need to worry about. What about Tyson and Daphne?"

"I'll take care of us," he promised.

"We never even knew or suspected we were being watched."

A reminder of his failure. "I'll move back in."

"That won't solve anything. You know we need more than that."

He did, and it pissed him off. "What makes you think shaking dog paws will keep us safe?"

"I don't, but I have no other ideas. Do you?"

He hated to admit. "No."

"Daphne is too little to defend herself if *they* come after her."

They didn't need a name. *They* stood for the faceless doctors and their minions who would take them into custody and put them in windowless rooms.

"They better not dare," Stefan growled.

"If they're the ones watching, we're in so much danger. Those people dared to order your death."

"I know." Since Stefan heard about it, he'd been having nightmares every time he closed his eyes. Memory or imagination? He couldn't know when he woke up with his heart racing.

"Just like you also know we can't afford to say no to the only people with the means to help."

"What does pledging allegiance entail? A ceremony during the full moon?" He was only half joking.

"Actually, Gwayne suggested a wedding." The bomb dropped. It took a shell-shocked second to reply.

"Out of the question." The exclamation burst from Stefan. He didn't even ask who they wanted to barter off. No one in his family would be sold like merchandise. "I can't believe they'd even suggest it. I'm going to give that fucker a piece of my mind."

"Stefan, maybe you should think about it."

"Think about what? That he wants to force Ray or Jessie? Fuck, what if it's Maeve? She's too young. And we both know Pammy's not into marriage with a dude. This is bullshit."

"Is it? I personally think he's serious. He's offered his sister as the bride."

For a second, he pictured himself as the groom, only to remember, given his issues, he never planned on getting married. That narrowed it down to Raymond or Daeve. Neither acceptable. Stefan's sudden rage blinded him. "I gotta go, Mom."

"Stefan, wait, there's more."

"I don't want to hear it." He hung up.

Time to tell this alpha wolf where to shove his demands of fealty.

12

NIMWAY HEARD THE MOTORCYCLE AND thought nothing of it. Frank up the street drove a Harley anytime the weather looked clear.

The raised voices did bring her out of the office to see an unwanted visitor standing in the front hall, arguing with Percy.

"What do you want?" She scowled at Stefan, the one person she didn't want to see.

"To see your brother. Now," Stefan snapped, his irritation as fiery as his hair. Stefan held his motorcycle helmet in one hand and appeared unhappy to see her.

What an asshole.

"I tried telling him he had to call ahead first." Percy had only angled his body enough for her to face Stefan. He wouldn't budge, not with Stefan acting aggressive. As If she needed his protection.

"I don't have time for this bullshit. I want to speak to him now."

Now was it?

"Aren't you demanding." She waved to Percy. "I got this. Get the crew going." Only once Percy was gone did she snap, "What do you want?"

Rather than answer, he asked a question of his own. "I thought this was your brother's house."

"It is his place. I live here as his roommate. Is that a problem?" She arched a brow.

"No. Where's your brother? We need to speak." Still no hello. Not one single soft word that would pay homage to the kiss they'd shared.

She crossed her arms. "Do you have an appointment?"

"No."

"Then that explains why he's not here to bow to your incredible rudeness at barging in."

That brought a scowl to his handsome face. "Where is he?"

"Not here." She enjoyed the way a muscle ticked high on his cheekbone.

"When is he coming back?"

"Do I look like his secretary?"

"You're too damned hot in those jeans to be a secretary," he growled.

Like literally growled.

And it was sexy.

She ignored it. "Exactly what do you think my brother does all day? Hang around his house doing nothing?"

"Isn't he your leader?" Spoken with a sneer.

"Even an alpha has a job. The bills don't magically get paid." Although they could if needed. The pack had the funds to help those who fell on hard times, usually under the guise of hiring them for some bullshit job. But hiding in plain sight meant doing the mundane things other people in suburbia did, such as going to work, earning a paycheck.

"So he works while you stay home." He seemed determined to fight. Who'd pissed in his cereal this morning?

"I have a job."

He glanced at the door. "That requires muscle for protection?"

The misassumption brought her laughter. "Yes, but not for the reason you think. Percy is part of my roofing crew."

He blinked at her. "Your what?"

"Remember the part where I said I have a job? I run a roofing company."

"Like fuck." He glanced at her hands.

She held them up. Clean, but rougher than most ladies'. "These days, I do more of the paperwork and customer service shit than I like, but in a pinch, if we get shorthanded, I know how to layer on asphalt shingle and spread tar."

"If you're a roofer, how come you're wasting daylight?"

"By law. You do realize it's only seven thirty in the morning."

He grimaced. "Don't remind me. My mom woke me at the crack of dawn."

"And why, pray tell, did she do that?"

"Because your brother called her."

That surprised and didn't. After their argument last night, she'd hoped for more time. She should have known better. "And what did your mom and my brother talk about?" Judging by his anger, she could guess.

"Don't play stupid. You know your brother wants some kind of oath of allegiance from my family."

"Hardly a travesty."

"It is if we're not interested."

"And do you speak for your whole family?"

His lips pressed into a line. "I'm not a fool. We both know your brother went after my mom on purpose. Made her think there's no other choice for our family than to join your pack." His tone left no illusions as to what he thought of that idea.

"My brother spoke to your mom because she's obviously the smart one in her family who understands you have few choices," Nimway snapped. "Here are the facts. This is wolf territory, and while you managed to slide under our radar for a few decades, it doesn't change over a century of us living here. This is our land, and you are a threat."

"Like fuck we are."

"Actually, you are, especially given what recently happened with your brothers. Their antics have put us all at risk."

"It wasn't Ray's fault. Someone spiked the chocolate."

"Yes, and that person has been taken care of."

"Meaning what?"

"Meaning they won't do it again, but there are other threats that need to be handled. Or have you forgotten the people watching you?"

"According to you."

"Yeah, according to me. And it's me who's going to have to make sure they don't catch your family and expose us all."

"I want to help." He flexed his fists; his face took on a violent cast. Along with that motorcycle jacket, he oozed sex appeal and made her want to do bad things to him.

She stayed focused. "Unfortunately, that won't be possible. You're not pack. We don't let outsiders into pack business." She knew the statement would goad him.

"Except this is *my* family's business."

"That is in *our* territory," she mocked.

"It is way too early for this shit."

"Not a morning person, are you?"

"I run a night club. Thursday to Saturday."

"No wonder you're like a frat boy at times."

"Accusing me of being useless?"

"More like a cry-baby, actually." She purposely goaded him.

However, rather than get angry, the man softened, took a step toward her, and smiled. "I guess I am coming off as complaining. When woken too early, I get a bit grumpy. Let's start over. Or maybe we should continue where last night left off?"

Wait a second, flirting? Now, in the midst of a fight? Did he think that would work? That her panties would get wet—they did—and she'd just melt in his arms?

Unbelievable.

As he reached for her, she stepped away and shook her head. "Oh no you don't. I am not some little sex doll you can turn on and off at will."

His lips twisted. "It was worth a try."

"Seducing me won't get your family out of your obligations."

That quickly, he was ranting. "We don't owe your pack shit."

"Whine. Whine. That's all you do," she huffed, rolling her eyes.

"Just because you're all good at bending knee to your brother doesn't mean me or my family will."

"Actually, I'm going to guess you're the most reluctant."

"Understatement," Stefan muttered.

"Which is why my brother proposed the idea of using marriage." At first, she'd been adamant. No way. It was barbaric. Archaic.

She'd defy her brother's command. For once, she'd be selfish and ignore the needs of the pack. She'd stomped away telling her brother to shove his arranged marriage where the sun never shone. But in bed, the benefits occurred to her. And what of the pleasure?

"No one is getting married." Stefan sounded firm on that point.

Her turn to be persuasive and perverse just because he said no. "Why not? It solves so many problems at once. One, no need to figuratively bend the knee because the marital alliance creates an instant bond between our two families. Two"—she flicked another finger—"it extends the pack's extensive protection to you. Although the location of your family home might have to shift. It's a little remote to defend properly."

"Mom isn't moving."

Again, his bald statements didn't match what she knew. "Are you sure? Magda, who had a long chat with her last night, says your mom was talking about how she's getting older and wouldn't mind downsizing. It's a lot of land to maintain, and the house keeps falling apart."

"So we fix it. It's our home."

"Home is where the head rests at night. And we have a lovely one that just came on the market. Safe neighborhood, excellent school, walking distance to everything, including medical services."

"We don't need…" He paused. "You want us to move so you can keep us under your paw."

"You and your condo are fine. Adults are expected to take care of themselves. We're talking about your mother and the younger children."

"You want to stick them in a house where you can control them. Like slaves."

"Hardly slaves. Think of it as a benefit to our alliance."

"Whoring someone out, even under the guise of marriage, is gross and not a prize."

"Unless it's in name only," she suggested.

"Ha, as if I'll believe that. No one is marrying my sisters and molesting them."

"Didn't you hear? I'm the bride, and I was thinking more of joining with a brother." She tapped her chin.

He looked angrier than ever. "You're okay with being sold off? And here I thought my mother was bullshitting. I've met you. No way is anyone forcing you to get married."

"Who says I'm being forced? It occurs to me that having a husband could be useful to me, especially since my brother will then stop harassing me about the creation of an heir. I am not a breeding heifer," she grumbled. "An arranged marriage in name only will put an end to that kind of talk."

"Wait, you're saying you want to get married so you don't have to have a baby?"

"Kind of hard to get pregnant if no sex is involved."

His brows hit the ceiling. "You can't seriously expect someone to marry you and give up sex forever."

The statement proved interesting. Did it mean Stefan believed in monogamy if committed? And that she was sexy enough that hands-off wouldn't be feasible? He'd certainly been hands-on the night before.

"It would be an open arrangement that would require extreme discretion because my brother might not be as open to the idea if he were to find out it's a sham."

Stefan turned stony. "And which of my brothers are you meaning to fuck over? Pretty sure Anika would have a problem with Dominick dumping her to hitch himself to another chick. And you can't have Ray. You'd eat him alive."

"There is another."

"Daeve isn't interested in what's between your legs."

"I wasn't talking about him."

His brow furrowed. "Tyson is only sixteen."

"Not him either. Think hard, baby. Who else is of marriageable age in your family that might not mind getting a meddling mother off his back, who would avoid having to kiss any feet, and would get automatic standing in the pack?"

"Me?" His brows left his forehead. "Never! Like fuck. I won't do it."

"Goodness. Temper. Going to pound the floor next and cry about life being unfair? Maybe throw some things? I'd start with that statue over there. It's pretty much shatter proof."

He glared. "You're not funny."

"And you're supposed to be an adult."

"Nothing childish about my anger."

"Actually, it's getting boring. So let's finish this once and for all. Will you marry me, Stefan Hubbard, and align with my pack, or are you going home, putting up a for-sale sign, and getting your ass out of our territory?"

She truly expected him to go stomping out that door.

Only the man never did what she expected.

He grabbed her and dragged her to him, murmuring against her lips, "Oh, I will marry you, darling, but on one condition only. There will be sex. Lots of it."

13

IT WAS FUCKING CRAZY. STEFAN HAD AGREED to marry Nimway, a wolf who drove him nuts—with passion—but if he did, he'd damned well fuck and lick every inch of that delectable body.

She'd been adamant, though, about making it in name only. He waited for her argument. Her laughter even. Anger.

Nimway said, "Fine."

Just fine and it was enough for him to kiss her, passion flaring even faster than before. How was it his clothes didn't catch on fire?

He held her tucked tight to him, hands firm on her ass, grinding her against him. She hummed into his mouth. Moaned her acceptance. Her need.

But when he would have taken her right there in

the hall, she put a stop to it. "Not until you put a ring on it."

Words to make any man run. It should have sent ice through his veins. Ignited his self-preservation. How many times had he mocked those who willingly chose a ball and chain?

Madness, yet he did nothing to stop it. Rather, he kept them both aroused with her on his lap as she sent some texts that ordered her crew to work without her. A few phone calls and emails later—and him hard enough it actually hurt—she'd arranged everything. They didn't have to wait the usual time period. Nimway apparently knew a guy who knew a gal who could process a license for them within hours.

With copies of their identification and paper-work, they zipped downtown in front of a judge and repeated their vows. A good thing no one gave him a quiz right after to ask any of the details. He only had eyes for her.

His bride.

Then, suddenly, his wife.

They were married before lunchtime. The very speed of his reckless decision had him dazed. But that didn't stop him from accepting the key to a lavish suite at Chateau Laurier, rented to them with a crazy surcharge for early entry.

They could have asked for more, and he would have paid. Anything to ease the pressure inside.

Nimway had the keycard and led the way, that sweet ass swinging. He loped for her and swung his bride—who wore a pair of white jeans, a fluffy cream sweater, and big hooped earrings—into his arms, startling her.

"What are you doing?"

"Carrying my bride. Isn't it tradition?"

"It's supposed to be over the threshold."

Rather than reply, he kissed her. Properly this time, given the one in front of the judge resulted in cleared threats and a demand they move along.

It was torture to have her clinging to his back on the way to the hotel, snug against his back as he drove his bike. If the hotel had been any farther, he might have found an alley.

To think she'd imagined she could ask to marry him and not expect him to touch her. She was that freshly frosted cake that begged a finger to take a swipe. Something that just couldn't be resisted.

He kept her in his arms as they entered the elevator, her weight as if nothing. She clung to him, making them one being, one desire. A good thing they arrived quickly, or someone might have seen the doors open on something that was far from PG-13.

Somehow avoiding bumping into the walls, he navigated to their room without dropping her. As a bonus he also didn't smack her off a hard edge or lose contact with her lips.

She was the one to slap the keycard against the lock as she turned the handle. Only once fully in the room, with the door shut, a do-not-disturb hung on the handle, did he set her on her feet.

"Carrying me over the threshold. How traditional," she teased.

"Says the woman who appears to be wearing old pearls and a new sweater. All that's missing is the blue."

She nipped his jaw as she whispered, "What color do you think my panties are?" Then lower and huskier, "Husband."

Fuck me. It hadn't been real thus far for him. Not when he filled out paperwork. Nor in front of the judge either. But she'd called him husband. Wore the ring they'd bought on a whim at the first jewelry store they entered, white gold band with a topaz stone.

On her ring finger.

Too late to turn back. Nor did he want to.

My wife.

His mind went numb, but his hands knew what to do as they stripped her. The clothes came off. No hesitation. Just pure frantic need on both their parts.

Hands skimmed skin. Lips locked, and when they parted, tongues played. Stumbling, they somehow managed to find the bed. Nimway landed on her back, him atop her, framing her. His erection dangled heavily between his legs. He wanted nothing more than to fuck her.

To drive into her until she screamed his name.

Yet, he paused because he could smell her arousal.

Actually scent her sexy musk. His mouth craved a taste. A touch at the apex of her thighs and his fingers met her honeyed wetness. He licked his fingers.

"Mmm," he hummed as he met her heavily lidded gaze.

Her swollen lips parted. "More." An invitation that came with a wiggle of her hips.

Hell yeah, more. Using just the tip of his cock, he rubbed her clit, watched the fat head of it stroking, making her squirm. He could see the petals of her sex, her pubes kept short but more than a landing strip, which he liked.

He slapped his cock off her clit a few times. She bucked, and her back arched, drawing attention to her tits. The berry-like nipples beckoned.

Bracing himself on his forearms, he kept his cock positioned to rub and friction her clit so he could lean down and capture a tip in his mouth.

She uttered a long moan.

Nice.

With the flat edge of his teeth, he lightly grazed the tightening nipple. It shriveled, and he sucked it.

Nimway panted, her hands fisting into the coverlet of the bed, arching and pushing the globe farther into his mouth, and he eagerly sucked.

Tugged.

Pulled with his mouth as she cried out. He swirled his tongue around the taut nub. Bit down while his erection teased her. He almost lost it when her legs lifted to wrap around him, locking him between her thighs, trapping his dick between their bodies.

"Fuck me, husband," she taunted. "Fuck your wife."

The words only served to thicken him further. He angled until the top of his engorged head parted her nether lips.

Her legs tightened around him, drawing him deep, sheathing him fully. Completely. Perfectly. Stefan uttered a moan and then a groan as her slick muscles tightened around his shaft. She squeezed him, and he almost lost it. He pulled back then pushed as deep as he could to sheathe himself. Nimway tilted her hips and quivered.

Stefan pulled out, right to the tip, and then thrust deep. She grunted.

He thrust again. Finding that same sweet spot.

Over and over he pounded it as she cried out and clawed at his back. Urged him harder. Faster.

He couldn't help but obey, grinding against her, making her keen in pleasure, the sound intensifying until, with a choked scream, she came. And he came with her.

He realized only too late they'd not used protection. Nor had they discussed what would happen after the ceremony.

But he did know one thing. He'd married this woman and consummated, making her his legit wife. Until death do us part.

It felt right.

As he kissed her, he hardened inside and started moving again.

She squeaked. "Already?"

Yes. And while it took a bit more work to bring her to the edge, it was soul-shuddering good when she came, screaming his name, nails dug into his back.

Two orgasms down, they lounged in bed, eating from the room service tray they'd ordered. A shower led to round three and them lying in the bed, naked, with their limbs entwined.

They'd yet to talk, as if neither wanted to ruin this idyllic moment, but they couldn't remain silent forever. Maybe, though, they could have one fantasy day before dealing with reality.

Just as he debated running them a bath, his phone rang and rang.

Mom's ringtone.

He ignored it. Naked in bed with his wife was not the time to be talking to his mom. Especially since Mom would lose her shit she hadn't gotten to attend the ceremony.

It stopped only for a second before it started again.

It could mean only one thing.

Trouble.

14

STEFAN'S BODY TENSED AS HE ANSWERED the phone. He didn't start with the pleasantries but went right to the point. "What's wrong?"

"Tyson is missing." A panicked rush of words from his mother that Nimway heard easily.

She sprang into motion. She grabbed her phone and fired off a text to the pack hub, *Tyson Hubbard. Location.*

As she waited, she kept an ear on Stefan.

"What do you mean missing?" Stefan exclaimed as he rolled out of bed, lean and sexy. He activated the speaker before tossing the phone onto the bed. He needed his hands to fumble on his clothes.

"I don't know where he is!" His mom huffed hotly.

"Then what makes you think he's gone?" Stefan

paused, shirt in hand as he waited for a reply. The eye candy was fun, and she ogled it.

"I received a text that said *Kids in danger. Keep inside.* Only I didn't see it until too late. Tyson had left the house, and he's not answering his phone."

"It could be someone screwing with you," Stefan suggested.

"What if it's not? What if—"

The voice cut off abruptly. "Mom? Fuck. The line dropped." Stefan frowned at his phone. "That's weird. No signal."

"We can be there in twenty minutes if we move," she said, finishing dressing. She'd yet to receive a text back from the pack hub.

"Fourteen if I don't hit any lights or disturb cops." He slid on his shoes as she tried to send a new text.

It failed. No signal. Maybe they were in a bad service zone.

A stony-faced Stefan uttered a dry, "I swear, if that boy's off smoking catnip again, I will beat him to within an inch of his life."

"Has he ever disappeared on your mom before?"

"Only that one time. Fuck me. I hope it's something dumb like the kid getting high."

"We'll find him."

"We who?"

She almost rolled her eyes and reminded herself

he'd yet to truly grasp how the pack worked. "The pack will help find him."

"He's probably in the woods," Stefan remarked as they exited the room.

Yet, he couldn't completely hide his anxiety that something might have happened. She could only hope it was benign and that Tyson hadn't been taken because that would make things complicated. Surely the text the mother got was a joke. The hub would trace it, and the prankster would get a stern talking-to.

She glanced at her phone. Still no bars.

The elevator opened almost as soon as they jabbed the button. As they boarded it, others already inside the cab were muttering about their phones and the lack of signal. Nice to know they weren't the only ones, even as it annoyed to be cut off. She'd not realized how much she depended on her phone, on being connected. They were moving blind.

As they left the hotel, people in the lobby and at the front desk were exclaiming over the widespread service interruption, city-wide apparently. A sign of something nefarious afoot? How hard would it be to disrupt cell service and internet? No idea, just like she had no clue if there was a coordinated effort to come after them. Nimway couldn't call her brother to warn him, not even to reassure herself. What if he needed her?

Stefan needed her, too.

Pack or husband?

Wasn't Stefan pack now?

The decision tore at her, but she knew what she had to do.

Nimway clung tight to her new husband as he raced from downtown Ottawa to Richmond. No fear as he took some corners leaning. She followed his lead, and they were one with the machine, so in tune with each other it was uncanny.

Was that why she'd married him? Because she'd been firmly opposed when her brother suggested it. Told him to take his idea and shove it, only to turn around and pretty much arrange the whole thing. She'd pulled in favors and done the unthinkable. She didn't just marry him…

I slept with him, too.

Actually, no sleep was involved. She'd fucked the shit out of him with no protection.

And she would fuck him again, because, damn it, why shouldn't she be allowed to enjoy it? Although she did feel a little guilty. While they'd been baptizing that motel room with orgasms, his brother might have been abducted. If the anonymous text could be believed.

Could the boy be fucking with them? Playing a nasty prank? If that were the case, he'd deserve a whooping. She knew in the pack that kind of thing wouldn't go unpunished.

What if it were real, though? What if the boy had been taken? What if the entire Hubbard family was in danger? After all, if someone had the balls to kidnap one kid, why not all of them?

The very idea chilled because the Hubbards could expose the pack, putting them all in dire danger. Dear God, it made her feel ill to realize that the emergency evacuation they'd prepared for all their lives might finally come into play.

This was why she clung to her husband as he raced home. She had to find out what happened with Tyson, hoax or threat, and then make sure the pack could proceed with the right information.

As they pulled into the driveway, she noted the light blue minivan, purple Jeep, and a Hyundai four-door sedan in gray parked out front. Before the bike even stopped in front of the house, the eldest Hubbard ran out the door, her face tear streaked.

"Stefan!"

"I'm here, Mom," Stefan said, yanking off his helmet. "We're going to find him. Where is everyone?"

Through a voice rough from tears, Nanette Hubbard said, "Dominick is in the woods with Maeve. Raymond is in the basemen yelling about bugs. I've got Anika sitting with Daphne and Pammy. Pammy's a mess."

Their older sister wasn't the only one.

"Tell me again what happened." Stefan had reached his mother and grabbed her hands, steadying her. It didn't help the woman had already given in to full-blown panic.

"I don't know," she wailed. "One second, Tyson got home from home from school, and the next, he's taking his bike through the shortcut to meet the boys."

"What shortcut?" Nimway interrupted.

Stefan pointed behind him to the woods. "You can cut off almost half a kilometer to the corner store by taking the path through the forest."

"He does it all the time. And it's only been an hour since he left. I didn't think anything of it," Nanette admitted, hanging her head. "I wouldn't have even worried for another few hours except I got that message."

"Can I see?" Stefan asked.

Nanette handed it over, the text already loaded. Simple. To the point.

Kids in danger. Keep inside. From a private number.

"It is rather vague," Nimway pointed out.

"She's right, Mom. This sounds more like someone fucking with you than anything."

"Then why isn't he answering his phone?"

"Probably because they're down right now?" Stefan suggested.

"I'm telling you something is wrong," Mrs. Hubbard wailed.

Never underestimate a mother's gut feeling. Nimway knew better, but she still had a duty to ask the right questions. "Is he the type of child to prank?"

The mother shook her head. "Not for something like this."

Stefan, though, rolled his shoulders. "You can't be sure, Mom. I mean look at the trouble you've had with him. The dope smoking. Vaping. The drinking."

"Teenage stuff. Experimenting is normal."

"Fine, I'll give you that, only he's also getting into fights at school, and he got caught shoplifting."

Mrs. Hubbard looked miserable as she whispered, "He says he meant to pay for it."

"You don't put stuff you're planning to buy in your pockets, Mom, and you know that."

The woman's head drooped. "He's acting out, yes. But he's a good boy. He wouldn't do something like this."

For some reason, Nimway believed her, and if it were true, and he'd been taken, then time was of the essence. "How long since he went missing?"

"I don't know exactly. It wasn't long after he got home from school."

"And you say he went in the woods?"

Nanette nodded. "With his bike. He does it all the time."

"We should be able to track him then."

"That's what Dom and Maeve are doing. They got here five minutes before you and took off right away. Raymond was going to use his drone but then started yelling at his computer. Apparently, the internet is down."

"Which is why he's freaking." Raymond relied on his network to be his eyes and ears.

A car pulled into the driveway, and two pack members spilled out. Nimway waved at them and shouted, "Are your phones working?"

"No." Dayna was in the lead. She waggled her handheld device. "Been trying to contact hub, but our lines are down. We happened to see you flying by during our turn on watch, which is why we came to see what's up."

"Tyson might be missing. Have you seen him?"

Dayna shook her head. "Not on our stretch of road. We did see a few school buses go by, though."

Nimway's lips pursed. "We need to find him. He was last seen going into the woods wearing..." She glanced at the elder Hubbard.

Nanette composed herself enough to say, "Red hoodie, black jeans, and his Sens ball cap. His bike is fluorescent green."

"Do you have something he's worn recently?" Nimway asked.

"His gym bag is in the front hall," Mrs. Hubbard replied, wringing her hands.

"That would be perfect."

Stefan ogled Dayna and Jack as they stuck their faces right into the smelly bag of clothes. Without saying a word, they trotted off for the woods on two legs. They knew what to do. She'd join them in a moment.

"Are you staying here with your mom in case he comes back or coming with me?" she asked her husband, given he showed no signs of moving. "You don't have to. If three wolves can't track one boy, then we shouldn't call ourselves hunters."

He looked tense as he said, "You're going to change into wolves?"

"We'll scent better and move faster in that shape. If you're coming, I suggest you do the same and shift into your tiger."

"Change? Like fuck." He shook his head. "My tiger would be useless. I can't control it."

"So you've insisted before. It's probably because of the catnip. You can't drug yourself and expect to run the show. It's like being drunk."

"I can't morph without it."

She wrinkled her nose. They really did need to discuss his belief that only catnip could shift him.

But not this instant. "If you're not going to shift, then I guess that means you're staying here?" She might have sassed the last bit.

"I don't see what you think running around the woods will accomplish if he's been taken."

"It's better than bitching about it and doing nothing."

He pressed his lips into a line. "You think I'm useless."

"I think it's a miracle your family has lasted this long," she snapped, not sure why she was angry. She stalked off, feeling his burning stare against her back.

So much for their marriage lasting a day. At this rate, they'd be divorced by the morning.

15

Nimway strode off, angry and stiff. Stefan almost followed her. Instead, he lit a cigarette, while his mother scowled at him.

"That was rude of you. She is trying to help."

"Condoning returning to the addiction I finally have under control isn't helping me."

"Is catnip that much of a drug to you?" his mother asked, brow creased in concern.

"It's insanely addictive. And terrifying because you never know where you'll wake up. You don't know what you've done." Only dream-like memories that resembled nightmares if focused on too much.

"I never realized," his mother mused aloud.

"You weren't supposed to." Because he'd never told a soul. He'd tried to keep his demons bound tight.

"I wish I had known because you shouldn't have been alone suffering," Mom pointed out. "Which is why you should talk to your siblings about it. It might help them to deal with their own changes, and you never know; maybe it will help you, too."

"I don't know if I can." Dredging up the worst moments of his life. Admitting the lows he'd sunk to just for a high. He couldn't. Couldn't stand to see the revulsion and pity in their gazes.

"No matter what, we'll always love you. We'd never abandon you." Mom pressed her hand on his arm. "When will you realize you're not alone?"

He knew he wasn't. Not only did he have family he should have trusted with his secret, he also had a wife who'd gone into the woods looking for his family because he was scared. Scared because he had something within he didn't understand. A beast he couldn't control.

Maybe it was time he tried.

"I should get some soup ready for when they come back." Mom bustled off, needing to keep herself busy lest she collapse in panic.

Stefan lit a second cigarette off the first and stared at the woods, thinking. There was no point in another person running around inside those woods. If Tyson had been taken, they wouldn't find him. Meaning a search was kind of useless. They needed to figure out where he'd gone.

Usually, he would have had Raymond track Tyson's phone like they had the last time he went missing. But his cell still showed no service, meaning Raymond couldn't do much. All Stefan could do was hate his impotence.

Daphne emerged from the house, hugging a ragged stuffed tiger that Stefan had won for her the time she skinned her knee at the county fair. He'd cured her tears by throwing enough darts—and paying five dollars each round—until he could overpay for the striped critter, because only a tiger would do. A lucky guess, or did his baby sister know more than she let on?

"Is Tyson going to be okay?" Daphne had gotten too big for nap snuggles, but she leaned against him on the porch swing.

"Don't you worry. They'll find him." If he was out there. Kidnappers could have taken him anywhere by now. But where could they go with a reluctant teenage boy?

He almost missed what Daphne said. "The postman brought Tyson a big envelope today."

"Oh?" The statement took him by surprise until he remembered another package delivered to the house, a package with catnip for Dom. They'd never found out who sent it. "What was inside?"

She shrugged. "Dunno. He took it to his room."

Could it be important? "Did Tyson open it?"

"Dunno. He left like five minutes later. Which is weird, cause when we were walking up the driveway from the bus, he was saying he had homework to do before he could play online with Jeremy."

Wouldn't be the first time Tyson skipped doing it, though. "Do you remember if the envelope said who it was from?"

Again, another roll of her shoulders.

Could this be connected to his brother's disappearance? "Have you told Ray or Mom?"

She shook her head. "Ray was busy fixing his computer, and Mom was crying."

They rocked in silence for a few kicks of the feet before Daphne peered up at him. "Do you think the bad men got him?"

His heart stopped. "Why would you say that?"

Before she could reply, Mom came outside. "Daffy! There you are." Relief warred with panic in her voice. "I thought you were watching a movie."

"I didn't feel like it anymore," Daphne admitted, hugging her tiger tighter.

"Oh, sweetheart. I know you're worried. Come on. I'm sure Dominick and Maeve will find him." Mom didn't say it meanly. Didn't even direct it at him, yet the guilt hit him hard and fast.

He should be out there searching, too, but then he wouldn't have heard Daphne's story.

A mysterious envelope. It begged looking into.

Stefan went to Tyson's room, ignoring the Do Not Enter Or Die! sign.

This was a matter of life and death.

Upon entering, he saw many of the things he expected in his brother's room. Posters with sports stars. A few smaller ones of hot girls. The walls were painted red, white, and black. Colors for the local hockey team. Go, Sens, Go!

A scratch in a spot showed the pink layer underneath. Growing up, this had been Pammy's room, because Mom had insisted a young lady needed space away from smelly boys. She was right. The fart contests growing up did get to epic smelly proportions.

The attic didn't get converted until Dominick moved and insisted on sending parts of his paycheck home to help out. The kids insisted Mom take it over as a master bedroom suite with its own bathroom. The old master turned into another bedroom and lost a few feet. The bathroom on the second floor turned into two. Girls and boys. Guess which was grosser? But the one his sisters shared endured the most yelling. Women took their beauty seriously.

The bedspread was a patchwork collection of old clothes. The stuff Tyson would have outgrown. Mom always had a blanket going, using the clothes that couldn't be handed down but still had some life left to them to endlessly create patchwork blankets.

Stefan kept his in the chest in the living room for the nights he needed a hug.

A scan of Tyson's dresser showed nothing untoward. Cologne and deodorant. A hairbrush with an open jar of gel beside it. The dresser drawers revealed a brother tidier than expected. His clothes were not only rolled but organized by color.

"Should have known there was something up with the kid." Stefan did the same thing. A sign of the pacing anxiety within.

It wasn't until the bottom drawer that he paused. Jeans neatly rolled and upright, perfect for the grabbing. Except for the ones at the back sitting a little higher.

He pulled them out and found an envelope underneath. The contents proved to be freakier than the expected drugs. Pictures. Images that slugged Stefan in the gut because he recognized the place and yet didn't.

I've never been there. So why did his mind flash to a room with no windows but many machines and a medical bed such as the one the little boy in the picture was strapped to? A small child—no more than a few years old—with arms, legs, torso, and even head bound to a cushioned surface. Eyes closed.

Even that young, Stefan recognized Tyson.

Oh fuck. His stomach clenched. What sick bastard had sent this to his brother?

And worse, what did they know?

He rifled through all the images. On the back of the last one—of Tyson dangling from an elaborate exercise system—he discovered a hand-written note: *Answers?* Along with a time and an address.

Stefan glanced at the clock on his phone. Barely enough time to make it even if he sped.

He had to try.

He pounded down the stairs, startling his mom who exclaimed, "What is it? Where are you going?"

No time to stop. "Airport!" He ran for his bike and prayed.

Please let me reach Tyson before it's too late.

16

DESPITE SPLITTING UP IN THE WOODS, Nimway and her pack ended up skunked, as the boy's trail ended on a busy road. No way of knowing which way he went or how far. They also couldn't go any farther as wolves. They'd need to resort to more human measures. They sprinted on four fleet feet back to the house, pausing at the edge of the forest only long enough to shift and put on clothes. Nimway's phone still showed no signal.

As she neared the house, it was to be met by Nanette Hubbard wringing her hands. "Thank God you're back. You have to go after him."

"Who?" She blinked as she realized Nanette must mean Stefan. His bike was no longer parked in the driveway. "Where did he go?"

"He yelled something about an airport and took off just minutes ago."

She wanted to curse. "The airport." It made sense. If the boy were taken, then they would probably fly him out. "Did he head for MacDonald Cartier?"

"I don't know. Maybe?" Mrs. Hubbard chewed her lip.

Maybe wasn't good enough. Nimway knew of at least a dozen other smaller private airstrips, all within an hour or so from here.

She wondered if Stefan had a reason for suddenly aiming for the airport. "Mrs. Hubbard, did Stefan talk to anyone while I was gone?"

The woman sniffled. "Just his little sister, Daphne."

A conversation with the youngest girl, led to her discovering what Stefan had learned and why he'd moved so quickly. The envelope of pictures had been left on the bed. They turned Nimway's stomach, and the elder Hubbard, who'd followed her, turned white.

"Can I see?" Daphne asked with an innocence even hardened Nimway wanted to protect.

"No. Oh God no," Mrs. Hubbard exclaimed.

"Why not? I'm the one who knew about them." The girl pouted.

The elder blinked at the youngest. "And should have told me. Why didn't you?"

Daphne, a girl with big eyes, shrugged. "I didn't know it was important."

"Actually, you've given us the biggest clue so far," Nimway declared. With an address in hand, she barked orders at Dayna and Jack, who took off so quickly she forgot to tell them she needed a lift.

Before she could beg for a ride from Mrs. Hubbard, the matriarch said, "We need to tell Ray about this."

Nimway had forgotten about the hacker brother. "Is he downstairs?" She already knew he lived at home.

"Yes, he's been trying to track Tyson's phone, but he says Ottawa Valley is a dead zone for cell service right now. Something about some geese and a reception tower."

Fucking birds. They'd chosen a shit time to terrorize. "I need to talk to Ray." Then, because she noticed the eldest Hubbard on the edge of panic, one strung nerve away from snapping, Nimway offered distraction. "When we return with Stefan and Tyson" —because it was the only acceptable outcome— "we'll be hungry and thirsty. Shifting burns a lot of calories." A not-so-subtle hint.

Nanette Hubbard clung to that lifeline and

straightened. "I think we could all use a big batch of coffee and donuts to go with the soup I'm making." Stefan's mother bustled off to play domestic goddess, and Nimway shook her head, muttering, "That will never happen, husband."

"What?"

Nimway blinked at Stefan's sister. "Nothing." There'd not had a chance to announce the marriage yet.

It might never see the light of day given the unravelling of their lives. More and more it appeared as if they were compromised. The best thing to do would be to tell the pack to evacuate and leave the troublesome Hubbards behind. Abandon her new husband, with whom she'd already had a fight, to deal with their past alone.

Going to walk away the first time things are tough? her conscience chided. And more importantly, since when did she have a yellow belly? Someone threatened their existence. The Hubbards were now pack, which meant as beta, it was up to her to do something about it.

"Let's go find this other brother of yours," Nimway said to Daphne.

"Ray's in his cave." Daphne skipped ahead, leading Nimway down some stairs into a basement. It had been converted into an operations center, meaning lots of screens, a counter running around the room with keyboards, and other electrical apparatus. A treadmill sat against one wall beside a lone box marked DK then, with a different colored slash, *charity*.

"Ray-ray," Daphne sang.

"Not now, kind of busy," Raymond muttered, his hands moving joysticks that Nimway realized must control the camera on screen. Drone footage. Slick, but useless since the kid had already left the area.

"Might as well call them back in," Nimway advised. "Your drones aren't spreading out far enough. The boy is long gone."

"And you know this because?" Raymond asked, swinging around in his chair.

First, she pointed to the young girl. "You heard your mom. Look away."

Daphne offered her a solemn stare and said, "Why? I remember."

Dear God, had everyone in this family suffered? Outwardly, Nimway remained stoic, but inside, she raged at what had been done.

"Remember what?" Raymond asked. "Can someone explain what's going on?"

"Warning, these might be triggering." Nimway spilled the envelope of images.

The gasp that erupted from Raymond held shock

and pain. "Where did these come from?" Raymond spread pictures on the table with trembling fingers.

"Someone mailed them to your youngest brother." And Stefan had seen them. He'd left his smell all over the envelope and pictures. No wonder he left in a rush. She wanted to run, too, when she saw the images the first time. They hit like a well-aimed, powerful punch to the gut that also broke the heart.

The second time wasn't any better.

Peeking over Ray's shoulders, she had to bite the inside of her mouth lest she react. The child featured was clearly the one missing, the facial features similar enough, given they remained lean, the eyes unmistakable. Eyes that had seen too much.

Stefan wore the same expression. Come to think of it, they all did, a result of medical depravity that she'd not truly grasped until seeing the graphic images.

Raymond flipped the last one. Immediately, he began typing and mumbling. "The fucking airport, of course."

"Can you contact them and stop any outbound flights?" Because so long as the planes stayed on the ground, they could rescue Tyson.

"I'm going to try," he muttered. "The problem being, the major telecommunications services are down. I use a SAT system, but that small airport doesn't, making this difficult."

Raymond multitasked as if he had a number of hands and arms. She remarked on it quietly to Daphne. "He's like an octopus. How does he do it?"

The girl shrugged. "He's smart."

Having a few hackers in the pack, she recognized a good one when she saw it. Putting him to work for the pack would be a definite boon.

Within five minutes it became very evident he wouldn't succeed as he cursed and cursed some more. "I can't get through."

"Fuck! I need to get there. Maybe Stefan managed to stall them in time for Dayna and Jack to arrive." She tried to sound optimistic as they raced out of the basement.

Mrs. Hubbard saw them. "You've had news?"

"We're going to see if we can help," Ray shouted, snaring keys from a rack on the wall. "You should drive."

She held out her hand, and he tossed the keys before he jumped into the blue minivan. She sped out of there.

"You better hope he stalled them, or we could be shit out of luck finding them both," Ray said.

"You think they got Stefan?"

"If he got there before they took off, he's either been taken or worse. My brother might be many things, but he'd give his life for this family." The tires spun as they took off.

"He's not dead." She refused to think it for even a second.

"They might be better off," Ray said with a low grimace. "If they were both captured, I can only assume it was so they could be taken to a lab for testing."

"The same one that created you?"

"No idea. And before you ask, I don't know where it is. Mom never took any of us when she went on a voyage to bring home a new brother or sister."

"She took a big risk taking you all in," she surmised softly.

"She saved our lives while putting hers in jeopardy. None of us would be here today if not for her. Given the pictures Tyson received, they must have discovered the switch and hunted us down."

Nimway shook her head. "I think what's more likely is they've been watching and waiting to find people like you. Like us. When they spot a possibility, they go after them." The very idea sent a chill. Especially since they'd often scoffed at the movies and books where that kind of thing happened.

"Dominick's attack on Anika's ex drew their attention." Raymond rubbed his forehead. "If they suspected Dom, though, why go after Tyson? Why send those pics in particular? Wouldn't they have targeted Dominick instead? After all, the evidence of a shifter existing pointed to him."

Nimway's fingers clenched the wheel of the mini-van. "The bigger picture is if these assholes hurt them enough, then they will crack."

And none of them would be safe.

17

STEFAN DROVE AS IF HIS LIFE DEPENDED ON it. Being late because he'd not taken a risk? Not an option. His brother's safety hung in the balance.

The private airstrip was only fifteen minutes from Mom's place by car, longer by bike, which he assumed Tyson rode. Or had he called for a ride share? It didn't seem likely given the whole internet was down. Not to mention, the kid had given himself plenty of time to get here.

Like an idiot.

Seriously, what the fuck possessed his little brother to hop on his bike and meet some obviously sick people? Who the hell had sent what amounted to psychological torture to a child? To anyone for that matter?

Sick fucking bastards. Why would they do to his

little bro? He couldn't be late. Couldn't fail him. Not like he failed EK09. The memory had hit while he drove—had almost sent him crashing.

They were dangling from the bars again. High over the floor, one welded metal ladder lead into another, some of them angled up, others down. By the time he'd run the circuit a few times, his body ached. But he held on. Had to. Falling from this height would hurt.

"ST11. Why are you stopping?" The male in the white coat snapped the query.

ST11 knew better than to reply. They'd accuse him of insubordination. A big word he couldn't pronounce but understood to mean punishment.

"Can't."

The sharp cry had him looking down to see EK09 struggling. Panting. The muscles in her arms trembled. She was smaller than him. Smaller than many. She had difficulty on the bars.

The male in the white coat had a warning. "If you fall and break something, it's over for you."

Meaning she'd better hold on. ST11 started moving again, on a set of bars paralleling EK09's overhead.

He glanced down as he was about to pass her and saw her face. Red. Tense. Eyes wide and frightened. Her whole body shook. She wasn't able to move, leaving her only one choice. EK09 glanced down. It was far, and the thin padding would do nothing to cushion the impact.

He wanted to ignore her, but her plaintive cry had him

moving without thinking. He leaped down to the bar below and hit it, grunting a bit at the sharp impact. He scrabbled to get close enough to grab her wrists.

ST11 might not be as big as the man watching, but he was strong.

Her eyes widened, her mouth worked, and tears shimmered. He felt good about it as he worked to heave her to safety, perching her atop the bars.

The man in the coat said nothing for once but watched. Offered nothing as ST11 grunted and heaved at EK09. He pulled her through the gap, and she gasped as she grabbed hold and rested the weight of her body on the bars.

"Thank you."

What she said a second before the ladder-like bars tilted.

She fell. They both did. She died on impact, her eyes wide and staring. He broke his arm and, as a result, was tossed away like garbage.

He'd failed her. Failed them both. He couldn't let it happen again.

Stefan was almost to the small airport. It didn't have the same kind of security as a major hub.

It was four fifty-nine, one minute before the time on the picture. Not late by any means, and yet the place appeared closed. Not a single car sat in the lot. No Tyson. Nothing but a bike tucked against the building. A bike he recognized, as he'd bought it for Tyson for Christmas two years ago.

A part of Stefan wanted to shout for his brother, but his skin prickled.

Danger.

His brother must have arrived early.

Had they heard the bike?

Had he missed the meeting?

Too late to worry about that now. Stefan parked, kicking down the stand before swinging off the bike. He ran for the only door into the place. A tug on the handle showed it locked. A sign in the window read closed. It didn't open until the next morning.

If they weren't inside, then where?

The distant hum of a plane starting up caught his attention. It couldn't leave, not before he'd made sure his brother wasn't aboard.

Stefan moved around to the side of the building, noticing the aggressive chain link fence topped with barbed wire circling the place. The main gate had a massive chain and lock holding it shut.

Climbing it was, then. Trespassing was going to hurt. The fencing rattled as he used his fingers and the toes of his shoes to grip the holes. It was noisy as fuck. A good thing the engine noise probably drowned it out.

He dropped to the other side and only gave the briefest of glances to the empty runway. He aimed for the lights coming from the hangar with its bay door open. He angled away from that to the side, keeping to the shadows.

No one shouted an alarm, but that didn't mean he'd not been spotted. How many inside? What about Tyson? He couldn't let his brother be hurt.

How would he rescue him? His dumb ass hadn't thought to bring a weapon. Stefan was a decent fighter, but that wouldn't mean shit if they had guns. Guys who sent sick pics and asked to meet minors didn't play by the rules.

If Nimway were here, she'd advocate shifting. As if being a big cat would help if they had weapons.

It was going to be Stefan to the rescue and only Stefan because his phone remained incapable of making calls. Forget the cavalry. The odds didn't look good, and yet he had to try.

The side door to the hangar opened to his surprise. He quickly slid inside, his approach hidden by some pallets, shrink-wrapped and waiting for loading.

He edged along one and kept an eye out for any movement. There had to be somebody in here, or was everyone already on board?

Passing the line of cargo, he entered a wider area with a few planes parked. Small propeller types for the most part, but there was one sleek private jet with its ass end open and giving the appearance of having been deserted. Stefan highly doubted that.

All the hair on his body stood at attention. Warned him of danger. Told him to escape while he could.

If he left, they'd take Tyson. He knew it. Could almost swear he smelled his brother.

Somewhere.

Close by.

Probably inside that fucking plane.

A trap. He knew it, and yet he still had to look.

Stefan crept across the open space, aware he made himself a target, and yet what else could he do? Waiting might mean his brother was taken from him. He and Tyson might have their differences, but the love was very much there.

No one shouted or shot at him. Nothing moved at all. Meaning he could peek inside the cargo area of the plane. It took a blinking moment to grasp the fact he was looking at his brother in a cage.

Asleep, slightly tousled, and bent into a fetal position to fit. The fucking bastards.

He reached for the cage and began to tug. This close to the plane, the rumble of the engines made his teeth vibrate.

Which was when the gun poked him in the ribs.

"That's far enough. Let go of the cage and then turn around slowly."

No point in arguing with the person holding the gun.

Stefan released the cage and backed out, hands up, and turned to see a woman, weapon in hand, her brown hair pulled taut. Her clothes sleek and dark.

"Who are you?" he asked.

"Contractor." She smiled, that of a shark before biting. "The kind you should listen to when I say hands up and don't cause trouble."

His arms slowly rose. "Who hired you? What do you want with my brother?"

She arched a brow. "Me? I don't want him, but I am interested in the bounty attached to his safe return."

"Bounty." The word slipped from his lips.

"A bounty that just doubled with your arrival. Seems there are some people who will pay good money for the discreet return of their property."

"Nobody owns us," he snapped.

"They will once we deliver you both. You might not be worth as much, but since you're here..." She fired, and instinct made him dive low. The bullet missed him, and before she could fire again, he slammed into her, apologizing mentally to every woman he knew. Didn't matter she shot at him, his mama taught him to never hit a girl. But what about if that girl held a gun?

His assailant grunted as they hit the ground. He grabbed her wrist and slammed it against the floor, loosening her fingers on the weapon.

There was another shot, and a bullet hit him in the arm. He half turned to see a guy coming from another direction, readying his second shot.

Fuck. He stood and wavered on his feet. Eyes blinking.

Drugged.

No.

Instinct took over, and he ran for the second attacker.

Prey.

He leaped. A snarl emerged from his all too human lips.

The guy yelled as he fired.

Another drugged dart hit even as Stefan twisted. He swiped and missed. The woman who'd recovered didn't; she hit him in the back. Again and again. The many tranquilizers took him out.

Next time he woke, he was naked in a cell.

18

WHERE ARE YOU, BABY?

Nimway arrived too late. Her crew was in time to see the plane take off.

She might have let out a howl that sent every non-predator for miles around running.

The empty runway taunted. The vacant hangar with his scent enraged. The only clues left behind were Stefan's motorcycle and Tyson's bike. Where had they been taken? The tiny airport didn't have a departure board, and they had no idea where to look since the main office was closed.

Not that it mattered. Even once they managed to get through to someone, it became quickly obvious they were either lying or oblivious about what had happened at the small airport. And imagine that, criminals didn't file a proper flight plan.

Criminals didn't play by the rules, and she blamed the fucking bleeding hearts constantly giving them free passes. A society soft on crime saw it flourish. The pack understood rules and how necessary it was to uphold their laws. Laws kept them safe.

And see what happened when they got broken? A family of outsiders, who should have never been shown the truth about the pack, had been compromised and had put everyone in jeopardy. All because she'd forgotten the number one rule.

Only trust pack. Too late for regrets now. Nor could she lay all the fault at his feet. Stefan never wanted to be captured. She couldn't even blame him for coming after his brother without waiting. She'd have done the same. But him being taken along with Tyson was an extinction-level event for the pack. It was only a matter of time before one of the captured Hubbards cracked and said anything to save themselves.

Nimway did not look forward to telling her brother, her alpha, that their cover was about to be busted. The pack, everyone, would have to scatter, going into hiding until they could regroup somewhere safe with new identities. She already had her new name, Amelia Jenkins. Nothing close to Arthurian, yet she didn't look forward to using it.

When she arrived back at the farm, it was to see

more cars parked. Gwayne's dark-colored Yukon being the most recognizable.

Fuck.

With the phones still down, he must have gotten worried and come looking for her. After all, her last text involved the Hubbard kid.

The moment they parked, Gwayne was there, opening her door, yanking her out, and hugging her. "You're safe." His voice was gruff. His worry palpable. She was the only family he had left.

"You know what's happened?"

"Mostly, but I want to hear your assessment."

She gave him the bleak, unvarnished truth. "It would seem those who created the Hubbard children have come to retrieve some of them. Tyson and Stefan were abducted."

She heard a gasp.

"No." Nanette Hubbard rocked on her heels, looking shocked.

Nimway felt bad, and yet it had to be said. "I'm afraid it's true, meaning your entire family is in danger."

"And by that same token, so is the pack," Gwayne surmised with a sigh. "Fuck."

"Yup." She didn't know what else to say.

"This isn't good." He rubbed his face, looking tired and defeated. Another blow to a once-strong man.

"I know." Even more softly said.

Mrs. Hubbard wheeled around and headed for the stairs where some of the other children crowded. "If our cover is blown, I'd better get moving. It's been so long since I had a plan. I got complacent."

"I wish the damned phones were working," her brother grumbled. "I feel like we're stumbling around in the dark. We need to get the word out that we might have to disappear and fast. We'll have to split up and go house to house for the moment. I don't want to cause a panic, but we need to be ready."

He kept saying we, and all she could think of was Stefan being subjected to torture. Her mind blinked to those pictures, and she blurted out, "I can't help."

Gwayne paused before saying, "What do you mean you can't help? You're pack beta."

"I realize that; however, I need to handle something urgent first."

It took him only a second. "You want to go after the missing Hubbards."

"It's the smartest thing to do. If I can stop them from spilling secrets, then we won't have to relocate."

"It's dangerous."

"I promised I'd keep him and his family safe."

He snorted. "Circumstances have changed."

"More than you know," she muttered. And then,

because she couldn't keep a secret from her brother, she exclaimed, "He's my husband."

He stared at Nimway. "What?"

"Stefan and I got married this morning, and I promised him safety. Him and his family."

"A day too late."

She shook her head. "I can't just walk away. He's not only pack; he's my husband."

"And how will you help him?" Gwayne snapped. "These people obviously are ruthless with the means to take us out."

"Ruthless people with secrets or they wouldn't have resorted to such stealthy methods." If they were afraid to act openly, then it worked in her favor.

"What are you going to do? We don't even know where that plane was heading."

"She doesn't, but I do," Mrs. Hubbard declared.

19

MOM

THE DAY HAD COME. THE ONE NANA Hubbard had long feared. When they would come for her babies and steal them away.

She'd sworn to her brother to never reveal what she knew, and she'd kept that promise, partially out of respect to his memory, partially out of fear that the truth would come back to bite, but also because she never wanted her children to face the monsters that wanted to hurt them.

But now she didn't have a choice.

"They're in Alberta," she declared.

To which Nimway exclaimed, "Where?" A smart woman, with strength who might be able to help Stefan with his demons.

"There's no actual address for it, but I can pinpoint the general area on a map."

"That should be enough," Nimway mused aloud.

"You can't be seriously thinking of going," Gwayne declared. "The pack needs you now more than ever."

"You're right. They do. Because if I fail, their lives will be forever changed."

Her brother argued. "How will you get there? You hate flying."

Nimway shrugged. "I don't know."

"It's a long drive," Nanette advised. She'd done it enough times to know. But she'd not had a choice. People might have remarked on the woman flying alone with the strange children. "Days, so pack a bag if you're thinking of it."

"I don't have days," Nimway grumbled. "God only knows what they'll do to them if we wait too long."

Nanette had been trying hard to not let herself think the worst. "It's a good sign they took them alive."

"What makes you think they live?" Gwayne said before grunting as his sister punched him in the gut.

Nana couldn't help but wince. "Because why go through that kind of trouble otherwise?"

"That wasn't exactly warm and reassuring," Nimway grumbled.

"I didn't take you for the type who needed coddling. Wouldn't you rather know the truth?"

"Yes. But that doesn't mean I like it."

"Well, too bad, the truth is what you're getting," Nana said because, after almost a lifetime of lying, it would be nice to speak frankly for once. "I know a bit how this company works. They only get rid of those they consider defective. Anyone who fits their agenda is kept alive for testing."

"Is this testing pain-free?" Nimway asked.

Nana snorted. "I think you already know the answer to that."

"I can't see Stefan cooperating too well with that." Nimway's lips pressed into a line.

"I agree. Which is why if you're going, it has to be quick." Her boys were too stubborn to cooperate.

Johan had only ever managed to save those slated for death. Of the others? She'd never heard of any escaping. But then again, would Johan have told her?

She could only hope that her children, older and wiser, would hold on until she could find a way to rescue them.

Even if it meant exposing the truth to the world.

20

Nothing like waking up exposed to the world. Or in this case, those monitoring the cell Stefan found himself imprisoned in, naked as the day he was born. Or had he been poured out of some test tube? His inquiring mind really wanted to know. He might even find out given his current predicament.

He was strapped to a bed with Velcro restraints. The one on the left hadn't been done up as tight, which meant he wiggled enough he could pull free. In short order he stood up and glared at the bed then the room. By all appearances he'd returned to his first home, but with some upgrades.

Three concrete walls with the fourth one made of glass, thick enough that it didn't even vibrate when he punched it. Welded into it was a sliding door, which was locked. It didn't budge when kicked, shoved, and pried at.

They'd improved on the design. He remembered the place being dingier and the machines bulkier during his last imprisonment. Three years old when he'd been their lab rat. Only now did he make the connection that his nightmares were about him reliving his time in this place.

The memories spilled into him, none of them good. It sent him into a worried pacing that did nothing to soothe his churning mind.

Captured like a fucking idiot. Some fucking hero he'd turned out to be. Where was his brother?

Fuck, what about Mom, the kids, Nimway, her pack?

The thing he feared most, his deepest paranoia, had come to pass. Discovery and capture.

Stupid. Stupid. Stupid. He almost pounded his hands against his temples in his agitation. He knew it wasn't a good thing to do. Hitting oneself didn't solve anything. Neither did drinking or drugs. He needed all his wits to figure a way out of here. He also needed to make sure he didn't put anyone else in danger.

"You're awake sooner than expected." The voice came from above, and he glanced overhead to see dark glass, the kind behind which people could watch without being seen.

"Where am I? Who are you?"

"We've never officially met, although I was in charge of the first few years of your life. You might say I made you, given I hired your creator. Perhaps you've heard of him, Johan Philips?" The male's statement froze him.

"Never heard the name before," he lied.

"Really? Odd, given your mother was his sister. Then again, we didn't know him well either. Seems Johan wasn't the company man he portrayed himself to be. Why, look at the fact you're still alive instead of some long blown-away pile of ash. I'd begun to wonder if our monitoring of your family was a colossal waste of money."

The cold in his veins turned to pure ice. "You've been watching us? For how long?"

"We started only a few years ago when we realized Johan had left behind a sister with an unusual number of children."

"You spied on us."

"It's called observing an investment. And you should thank me for it. Initially I was going to have you all killed, but a staff member suggested we monitor you in case you had children that showed special abilities."

His stomach clenched. "You can't be serious."

"Do I seem like the entertaining sort?" The hidden voice sounded so smug.

"You sound like a man with a very small penis. The tiniest." In case it wasn't clear, he held two fingers very close together.

Dead silence followed by, "I am going to enjoy the tests, but you, ST11, will not."

A whirring was followed by a cabinet opening in the cement wall. The aroma hit him.

Familiar. Devil weed.

Stefan started to sweat. "No. I won't help you."

"As if you have a choice." More snotty amusement.

"Why are you doing this? Couldn't you have left us alone?"

"I could have but chose instead to recoup my investment. After all, you and the others in your family are company property." He kept talking about Stefan's family, nothing about Nimway and the pack. Perhaps all was not yet lost.

"You ordered us killed. Essentially putting us in the trash, which makes us fair game."

"I was ridding us of defective equipment, only it turns out you just needed a little tweaking. Odd how catnip is your trigger. It's usually an inhibitor in the feline pool. Which makes me wonder what your weakness is."

"I don't know what you're talking about." Probably dumb to lie at this point, but why make it easy?

The unseen voice made a chastising sound. "Are

you really going to play that game? Did you know we recently got our hands on your psych sessions? It wasn't easy, I'll tell you. They lost a bunch of their records during some virus that swept their server. But the doctor had the original paper notes."

Stefan went from icy to dead inside.

"Apparently in your sessions you discuss a delusion of yours that you imagined you were a tiger. The change was triggered by catnip of all things."

"You stole my medical file. Are there any lengths you won't go?" A rhetorical question.

"If you're trying to appeal to my empathic side, be advised I don't have one. The only reason you remained loose was because, at your age, you're of less use to us. We prefer our subjects younger. They're more malleable."

"What are your plans for me then since I'm old?" He wasn't dumb enough to think he'd just be released.

"I'm sure we can think of something. I know the scientists are eager to get samples from you both. And I am now very curious about your ability to father babies. We've had setbacks with other subjects."

That didn't bode well. "Fuck you. I have rights."

"Humans have rights. You"—a pregnant pause for effect—"you're nothing more than a lab rat."

The ominous statement had him pacing, looking

for a way out of the walls closing in. The more he strode back and forth, the smaller the room got.

"You can't do this," he growled, clenching his fists.

"I have, so best you resign yourself, or you'll discover what happens to those who disobey. Your collar is being tested as we speak."

"Collar?" Stefan's fingers went to this throat, and he swallowed hard.

"All pets should have one. It makes them less likely to wander off. Today's technology has made it so we never lose our subjects anymore."

The sly taunt had his nails digging into his palms. "I'll kill you."

"Actually, once that collar goes on, one wrong move by you, and zap, you'll be dead." The words sounded extra cold due to their faceless nature.

"Why are you doing this?"

"Because I can."

The speaker went dead, the channel turned off, leaving him alone to pace and rage. To wonder where his brother was. To wish he'd had a chance to say good-bye. To say I love you to his mom and his siblings.

His wife.

If only they'd had a chance to explore the passion between them. To bask in that domestic bliss that he scoffed in public but craved in private. To wake up with her by his side. For him to perhaps convince her to show him what her idea of being a shifter meant, because she appeared to embrace her other nature. Used it as a tool. She didn't fear it.

He flexed his hands. Stared at them. Remembering the videos he'd shot of himself back when the high was everything and he wanted to understand.

What he'd learned was morphing appeared impossible, even when he watched his home videos in slow motion. One minute a man, and the next, shit blurred, and a tiger appeared. A mindless beast with no thought about being seen and putting itself in danger. It liked to hunt. That was all he knew. And that if he wasn't careful, his catnip highs would kill him.

Was it any wonder he avoided it?

Yet, if there ever was a time when he needed to be strong and a fighter, it was now. He eyed the catnip in the wall.

Could he afford to lose his head? He needed to save Tyson.

The lid over the catnip slid shut just he noticed movement outside his window.

Too late.

The door to his cell slid open. A technician entered, pushing a trolley, shadowed by a guard who held a baton that Stefan would wager would give a shock. On the trolley was a collar.

Stefan retreated. "Stay away from me."

"Turn around. Hands above your head, palms against the wall," the guard ordered.

"Bite me, asshole. I am not letting you put that collar on." If it went around his neck, all chance at escape was done.

"You don't have a choice. We need to dope him," the guard said to the technician, who appeared bored as he pulled out a syringe and vial. As if for effect, Stefan got to watch him filling it and felt the fear trying to creep.

The door out of the cell remained open at their backs. Freedom if he could reach it. Doubtful, yet he had to try.

The technician squirted the needle, and as the guard smirked in reply, Stefan rushed them. The guard reacted quickly and swung, but his aim was off. The baton hit Stefan in the arm with a jolt that vibrated his teeth. He swung his fist, an upper cut to the guard's jaw that sent the guy flying hard onto his ass.

The technician gaped. Just for good measure, Stefan punched him, too.

An alarm went off, and the door whirred as it began to slide shut. He dove through the narrowing gap and heard the frightened exclamation of the tech locked inside before it sealed shut.

An alarm whooped, agitating those in the other

cells. The ages of the occupants ranged, as did their sex. Hands pressed to the glass, haunted expressions, they eyed him with resignation. The collars at their throats were a reminder of what awaited him if he didn't escape.

Could he leave without even trying to help? What of Tyson? Was he in a glass cage, too?

Stefan felt exposed and dumb running down the hall of cells, his dick and balls swinging. It helped those in the boxes were naked, too. Most eyed him with dull gazes, but a few cheered him on.

Little did they know he had no plan. Nothing. Nada. He wasn't a hacker like Raymond or a trained fighter like Dominick. Just Stefan, which meant, when he hit the end of the hall and when the guard emerged through the previously locked door, he hesitated.

The guard didn't. He lifted his gun, but before he could fire, Stefan jumped, a mighty spring into the air, possible because of the adrenaline coursing in his body. He flipped and landed in front of the surprised guard. Stefan snarled and batted his weapon aside.

Then he growled again as the guard dared to confront him. "Get out of my way."

The guard, with his broken nose and cropped dark hair, smirked. "You think you can take me, let's go. I heard about you. You need drugs to change. Ain't no catnip here, tigerman." A taunt that burned.

At the same time, it also reminded him of what Nimway had said. That he didn't need an herb; the ability was within him. He just needed to tap it. To flex that inner muscle that was his hybrid self.

How? Fuck, he should have learned to do this before. Confronting a guy who was stalling so backup could arrive wasn't the time to realize it would be useful to sometimes have claws.

The guard might have lost his gun, but he had a baton as backup. Stefan learned of it when it whacked him on the side and gave him a shock.

Ow. That hurt.

Fucker! He roared. The guy went to hit him again, and at the second blow, a different kind of pain and ecstasy took hold. He stretched and grew and changed and felt and...

Landed on the guard, who wasn't laughing anymore.

"Oh, fuck," the prey whispered. It then made the fatal mistake of trying to hit him.

A hard bite showed his prey the error of his ways.

A strident noise bothered. Time to leave this place. He butted the door in his way.

Turn the handle, idiot.

He put a paw on the lever and pushed. Locked. Of course. He eyed the electronic keypad. Even if he knew the code, how would he enter it? His paws weren't exactly fingers. Beside it was a black square with a red dot in the middle.

He glanced at the guard and noticed the keycard attached to his belt. He grabbed the clip with his teeth and snapped it free, eyed the pad, and stood to swing the card on it.

Green.

Click.

The door opened when his paw pushed the lever, but as escape beckoned, he paused. Eyed the cells behind him. They needed to escape, too.

I'm not a hero.

But he strove to be one.

Stefan dragged the body to the doorway with his teeth, wedging the door open. Then he grabbed the card and went after the cells. The key worked on the first five cells before it began flashing red.

No more opening doors. The first five cell inhabitants fled, but Stefan eyed the people left behind, looking for one in particular.

The alarm ceased screaming, and that annoying voice from before returned. "Stefan. You know it's useless. You can't escape. Return to your cell and you won't be severely punished."

"Rawr." He wasn't about to become a prisoner by choice. He trotted down the hall, eyeing the people within. Some looked human; some were not. Some were a mixture. All of them stared back at him.

Hopeful.

They shouldn't be. He'd failed.

"There's nowhere to go. I've deactivated the keycard. You might have gotten one door open, but the rest are locked down. You're trapped."

Then why was Mr. X yapping and sounding too calm?

The lights in the place glitched.

Interesting. Especially since the invisible voice forgot to turn off his microphone. "What do you mean we're not in control of the system anymore?"

Click. The sounds of many locks disengaging at once had him freezing in the hall, mostly because, at the far end, his little brother emerged with shell-shocked eyes and no clothes, but intact if one ignored the collar.

"Stefan? Is that you?"

Stefan understood him and even better had no urge to eat him, or anyone else spilling into the hall.

The lights flickered.

The elevator at the far end opened, and guards spilled out, spreading across in a row, armed with guns, giving them the advantage.

Until the lights went out.

21

Too late. Too late.

The words repeated themselves over and over in Nimway's head as the flight took its interminable time traversing the country. They didn't have the money or connections to manage a private jet to get them there fast, which meant going the traditional way, with a security check—"*Are you carrying any weapons, ma'am?*" Nimway lied with ease because they'd never guess how deadly she was. Especially with fear honing her focus.

They managed to scam only four seats on the first flight out. Gwayne remained behind to coordinate the pack's possible evacuation. Their future depended on what she found.

Raymond chose to come with her, as did Stefan's

brother Dominick and the sister with the interesting hair, Maeve.

The remaining Hubbards readied to leave their family home. Mrs. Hubbard maintained a stiff upper lip while packing her minivan with an efficiency that a drill sergeant would envy. But they would only move across town for the moment, into a rental Nanette had found online. Hiding in plain sight. It might just work.

Everyone had a plan but Nimway. Currently, the rescue operation consisted of finding the place. Then... she had no idea. The odds of confronting an enemy in its stronghold weren't very good, and her brother had called her out on it.

"You are walking into a trap," Gwayne said bluntly.

"Have a little respect for my skills, would you? I don't plan to saunter nonchalantly into enemy territory."

Her brother huffed. "I need you here, protecting the pack."

"I am protecting them." Because if the kidnappers knew about them, then no one was safe. What if they never got a chance to find out about them? What if everyone could be safe?

"I can't believe you'd risk your life for a man you just met."

Her shoulders rolled. "I know it's crazy, but it feels as if I've known him forever."

"Oh." Of all people, he'd know what she meant. Gwayne, too, had experienced it once upon a time.

"I have to do this."

"Come back to me, little sister." His tone tried for gruff and managed to border on the edge of broken.

She had every intention of surviving and bringing Stefan and his brother home. She just had no idea how. All they had was a circle on a map. A sizeable area that showed no damned roads. So weird and difficult to plan for.

If they wandered around too much, they'd be prematurely noticed. Their best bet was going in quiet, stealthy like. Infiltrate and extract the boys then exit just as quietly.

At least, that was the loose plan. They'd yet to hammer out the fine details, like where did Dominick plan to find this rifle he thought he'd be using? The airline wouldn't let him check one as luggage.

At least Raymond proved useful, getting feeds from satellites not accessible to the public. He'd managed to pull up actual footage of the area in question, and by zooming it down, they could see the thin thread of road that didn't appear on any map and was hidden quite a bit by trees. They even got a partial glimpse of a building that didn't exist in any registry.

When they landed, their rental awaited, a Ford

Explorer with buttons. Dominick kept pressing them. Raymond would rebuke and tell him to keep them optimized and push it back.

Maeve shook her head and muttered, "At least Daeve and me grew out of that." Daeve being the brother in the military.

"How far from the airport are those coordinates?" Nimway asked.

"Two hours." That they beat by thirty minutes going a little faster than was safe.

Cell service had been restored, and Nimway spent that time remotely dealing with panicked pack members, of which there weren't many. Most had known with the way social media and cameras exploded in use and popularity that it was only a matter of time before their happy neighborhood broke up. They were ready to move if needed.

Please let her not be too late.

It was Dominick who noticed it first. "Smoke in the sky." Especially significant given they neared their destination.

The road, which was more of a private drive, had nowhere to hide. But it was also too far to walk in with big open spots. They chose to be bold and kept driving right in. They soon saw the cause of the smoke.

"It looks like there's a building on fire." A low observation by Nimway.

Hard to be sure what it used to look like. As they neared, they saw people emerging from the smoke, stumbling and coughing, some heading for cars. A few supported each other; others emerged naked or wearing fluttering white gowns and collars. Those people ran away from the parking lot to the wilderness beyond. The most graceful escape being that of the antelope.

Nimway blinked. "Was that…"

"Yup." Dominick's one-syllable confirmation.

"I think we found the place," was Maeve's observation.

But where were Stefan and the boy?

"Pull over. I need to get out." Nimway tugged at the door, but it remained locked.

"We should find a more discreet spot. The cops and fire trucks are probably on their way."

"Don't count on it," Raymond muttered. "This place isn't on any of their radars."

The first of the escaping cars whipped past. Smart given the fire wouldn't remain contained in the building.

The explosion rattled the large SUV, and Dominick slammed them to a stop. "Fuck!"

Something inside had ignited, and the result? Flames licked at a tree, one of hundreds, thousands. Tinder waiting for just a spark to ignite.

And what did she decide to do?

"I'm going to find them." Nimway spilled out of the truck, ready to hunt, and she wasn't alone.

The Hubbards flanked her, dazed but determined.

"Which way?" Dominick asked.

"I don't know. Let's split up; we'll cover more ground."

The siblings went off, Maeve charging ahead first, the brothers spreading out from her. They concentrated on the area around the building where the heat proved most intense. Survival would send the smart ones fleeing to safety, away from the fire.

It took two sweeps before Nimway picked up Stefan's scent. After that, she tracked him easily enough, even in her human shape. He'd shifted.

She could smell the feline, musky and familiar. She'd know her husband's scent anywhere. The trail led her through the trees away from the smoke. Away from everyone.

When the scent stopped dead, so did her feet. She didn't need to look up to know where he'd gone.

"You going to pounce me, husband?" She glanced overhead as she said it. Saw him perched in the tree, a beautiful creature, his colors vivid, his lines lean and impressive. She might be wolf and him a cat, making him her opposite, yet there was no denying the powerful grace of the feline who leapt from the bough of the tree and landed before her.

She started to reach out a hand and paused.

Hadn't he claimed, when he shifted, he lacked control? That he became a blood-crazed beast?

She stared at him.

He stared back.

"Is that you in there?" she asked.

He cocked his head.

"Guess you can't answer. Can you shift?"

She'd swear he rolled his shoulders.

"How did you shift in the first place?"

He made a rawring sound. A low rumbly complaint.

"You have no idea, eh?" she mused aloud. Then she smiled at her tiger of a husband. "Better figure out how to shift if we're going to have that honeymoon."

Ever seen a tiger with a dropped jaw?

Epic.

But she enjoyed even more the sight of him changing suddenly, his body going from fur to flesh.

He gasped as if sucking in air after drowning and then croaked, "Holy fuck."

"Look at you, shifting like a pro."

He glared. "Ha. Ha. What the fuck are you doing here?"

"Saving you."

That brought a low growl to his lips. "Idiot. Why would you do that? You could have been captured."

Nimway arched a brow. "You mean like you?"

He offered a lopsided grin. "I escaped."

"And made sure others did too, I see."

"Not everyone." His lips turned down. "Things got chaotic once the fire started."

"Your brother?"

"First one I shoved out the door. I was following his trail in the woods when you started following me."

"We should find him."

"In a second." He drew her close and hugged her.

She hugged him back.

Maybe this marriage thing could work after all.

22

Stefan wanted to do more than hold his wife, but he remained conscious of the danger. The distant fire would grow all too quickly. He didn't want them trapped by it.

He tried to not be self-conscious about his nakedness. It helped his wife held his hand.

Hell, she'd fucking come looking for him.

And this time he hadn't failed.

He'd rescued his brother, and now he'd find him. An easier task than expected. The kid stumbled around the woods like he wanted to attract predators.

"Tyson!" He bellowed his brother's name and then had to suffer a hug, followed by a rapid, "Ew, dude, you're naked!" Whereas his brother had managed to steal some clothes on his way out.

"Give me your shirt."

"How's that gonna help?" the kid asked even as he stripped it off.

A few rips and Stefan wore it around his waist. Not the most epic garment, but he didn't feel as exposed as they ran back through the woods, the smoke tickling as they neared the spot Nimway insisted held their ticket out.

They didn't see anyone else in the woods, but he couldn't avoid hearing the occasional howls and yips or scenting the tracks of those escaping.

They made it to the truck, spotting his siblings on the way. Luckily Dominick had brought spare clothes, so Stefan didn't remain in his T-shirt skirt. He didn't have identification to get on a plane, though, so after assuring his mom he and Tyson were okay—and then reassuring Gwayne they hadn't spilled the pack's secret—Stefan and his wife decided they would drive back home. They saw his family off at the airport before starting a three-day trip that turned into a seven-day honeymoon. A few hours of driving and sightseeing, followed by fucking. So much fucking.

That turned into lovemaking somewhere just inside the Ontario border. Yes, lovemaking because it occurred to Stefan that he adored his wife.

Shocking, almost as much as finally arriving at the farmhouse and seeing it empty. Every trace of them was gone. The walls were even repainted. Despite them being safe, Mom was taking no chances. She'd moved the younger kids into town.

Which was where they drove next, white-knuckled all the way.

Nimway put her hand on his arm. "It will be okay."

"Like fuck it will. Not when she finds out what we did." Because Stefan still had yet to tell her. But Gwayne knew about the wedding, and Stefan had it on good authority Gwayne had blabbed.

"I'm sure it will be fine. So what if we got married?"

"Don't ever say that in front of her." Stefan worried it might be enough to make him a widower.

As they pulled into the house a street over from Gwayne's, he swallowed. "Maybe I should go in alone."

"Stop being a pussy." Nimway swung out of the car.

He caught up to her on the front steps. "If she grabs a knife, get behind me."

The door swung open before he reached it, and his mother beamed. "Thank God you're all right." Tears of joy brimmed.

He'd not expected that.

Stefan hugged his mother, glad to be home even if that home wasn't the house with the slanted floors that required tables to have custom-sized legs.

The warm and mushy moment didn't last.

"Ungrateful brat! Getting married without telling anyone!" she lamented.

He squirmed. "It was spur of the moment."

"We're your family."

"I—Uh—"

"I made him do it. I was worried he'd change his mind, so I dragged him in front of a judge." Nimway stepped in, and he waited for Mom to lash out.

Instead, she nodded. "That I can understand. He can be slippery, my Stefan. But he's a good boy. I'm glad he's found a partner who sees his worth."

Nimway smiled at Stefan. "Funny, because I would have said he sees me."

She'd told him on their voyage that she liked he didn't see her as weak. That he would argue with her one minute, not giving in just because she was bossy, and the next kiss her. Because he liked her authoritative nature. It didn't mean he'd fold to her demands, but he enjoyed her strength.

He especially enjoyed it later that night in the guest bed at his mom's house. He lay on his back with Nimway astride him, her fingers digging into his chest, her hips rolling and grinding as she pushed against him, taking him deep and biting her lip to avoid making the sounds that said he was rubbing her sweet spot. He bit his own fucking tongue it felt so good.

He doubted he'd ever tire of seeing her gaze shining as she stared down at him. A woman who'd chosen him over all others. A partner to stand by his side. A confidante with whom he had no secrets.

A lover for life.

He spooned around her when they eventually fell asleep. They awoke to an audience. His little sister Daphne to be exact.

"What's up, Daffy?" Stefan asked, his arm curled possessively around his wife.

"Mom says it's time to get up. Lots to do."

"Yeah, like job hunting," he groaned. He'd been absent one too many days, not to mention it might be best to cut ties with his old job just in case.

"Actually, Mom's cooking, and says she needs you to taste test."

"Taste test what?"

"Wedding cake. And you both need to be there," Daphne declared with a wag of a finger.

"Er, what?" Nimway was the one to balk.

"Oh, and you need to pick a color scheme." Daphne grinned. "Mom says you're not gypping her out of her dream wedding."

"But we're already married," Nimway uttered in a panic.

"Not until she gets to cry when you repeat your vows, according to her."

Nimway groaned, and Stefan chuckled as he nuzzled her hair and whispered, "Let her plan a second wedding with the trimmings. It will keep her from bugging us about kids."

Wrong.

Over the course of that day, where they ate different flavors of cake and Nimway was kidnapped to try on a bunch of dresses, while he was fitted for a tux, they were told they should aim for three kids, two boys and a girl. Nimway was also given a cookbook for beginners. For a second, Stefan worried she'd flee but instead she'd grinned. *"Better bump your life insurance and invest in some Pepto."*

That night, he said to her, "Fuck the wedding. If it's stressing you out, we can say no."

"Is this your way of getting out of our marriage? Hunh? You want to get rid of me?" Nimway growled as she crawled atop him and grabbed his shirt in two fists.

"Why the fuck would I want to do that?"

"I saw Lacey winking at you."

"Uh. I don't know who that is, and I don't care because I only have eyes for you."

And he'd marry her a hundred times if that meant they could have a life together.

EPILOGUE

THE DAY OF THE WEDDING DAWNED beautiful.

They'd decided to have it in the park surrounded by the houses.

This time, Nimway's something-old was Nanette Hubbard's wedding dress, which wouldn't fit for long, given what the doctor had told her.

Her brother gave her away, his eyes moist.

Even her husband looked a little misty and sounded rusty as he recited his vows.

Nimway didn't cry, but her allergies got bad a few times during the ceremony. She blamed all the cats, including her husband.

She did disappear at one point with Stefan, and people assumed the dirtiest thing. And they weren't completely wrong, but the nookie came after the report the pack hub had compiled about the burned-down installation.

It never existed. Meaning it never had an owner. And the people who fled it that night? Vanished.

It was as if the atrocities never happened, but the danger remained. Unlike Gwayne, Nimway wasn't so sure they should have aborted their plan to move out.

"Whoever was in charge knows the Hubbards exist," she'd reminded him.

"And they're afraid to act openly. I'd rather face the enemy in a place of my choosing, a place I know. Maybe instead of hiding, we should fight for our right to stay."

Fight for her home? Her family? Her husband?

The life within…

Stefan cradled her and palmed her stomach. "Anyone ever tell you that you're the best ball and chain a guy could ask for?"

"The last one to call me a heavy metal weight got cement shoes and went for a swim."

"Hmm, maybe I should ask for your forgiveness then."

"Or you could show me," she teased.

He showed her heaven three times. And when she was puking the next day, and she threatened to carve his balls, he held her hair.

Now that was love.

~

RAYMOND HAD BEEN KEEPING odd hours for most of his life. His mind worked in spurts, and when on a streak, especially one fueled by worry, he functioned on very little down time.

It meant that despite it being three a.m., he was awake when the text, addressed to him, dropped into a mailbox he kept on the dark web.

Raymond read it and arched a brow.

Stop poking. Or else. Signed, *Pink Llama.*

He replied. *Or else what?* Because any poking that caused a warning deserved even more attention in his books.

The reply came in the form of a full system shut-down, the kind that wiped his machines so that the only thing that appeared on his screen was a pink llama wearing sunglasses and a grin.

Game on.

WILL RAYMOND FIND THE HACKER WARNING HIM TO BACK OFF? AND WHEN HE DOES, WILL THE ANSWERS SHE'S CONCEALING LEAD TO A HAPPILY-EVER-AFTER?

For more information or books (including many HOT shifters) see

EveLanglais.com